NINETEENTH CENTURY
BRITISH GLASS

FABER MONOGRAPHS ON GLASS
edited by R. J. Charleston

NINETEENTH CENTURY BRITISH GLASS
(second edition)
Hugh Wakefield

IRISH GLASS
(second edition)
Phelps Warren

MODERN GLASS
Ada Polak

NINETEENTH CENTURY
BRITISH GLASS

HUGH WAKEFIELD

*Formerly Keeper of the Department of Circulation
in the Victoria and Albert Museum*

faber and faber

First published in 1961
Second edition, revised and reset
published in 1982
by Faber and Faber Limited
3 Queen Square London WC1
Filmset and printed in Great Britain by
BAS Printers Limited Over Wallop Hampshire
Colour origination by Keene Engraving Ltd
and printed by Ebenezer Baylis & Son Ltd
The Trinity Press Worcester and London
All rights reserved

British Library Cataloguing in Publication Data

Wakefield, Hugh
Nineteenth century British glass. — 2nd ed.
— (Faber monographs on glass)
1. Glassware — Great Britain —
History — 19th century
I. Title
748.292   NK5143
ISBN 0-571-18054-x

Contents

List of Illustrations   *page* 9

Foreword   11

Foreword to Second Edition   12

Acknowledgements   13

Introduction   15

Introduction to Second Edition   17

1. CUT GLASS   19

2. EARLIER COLOURED GLASS AND NOVELTIES   46

3. ENGRAVED GLASS   80

4. LATER FANCY GLASS   112

5. MOULD-BLOWN AND PRESS-MOULDED GLASS   140

Marks   160

Select Bibliography   162

Index   164

Illustrations

Where known, the location of the glasses illustrated is indicated in the captions. Glasses attributed to the Stourbridge Glass Collection and the Brierley Hill Glass Collection are in the care of Dudley Metropolitan Borough and housed in the Broadfield House Glass Museum, Kingswinford.

COLOUR PLATES

A. 'Gold enamel' glass plate, about 1837   *facing page* 64
B. Layered glass decanter by George Bacchus & Sons,
   about 1850   65
C. Painted water carafe from 'Summerly's Art
   Manufacturers', 1847   80
D. Silvered glass, about 1850   81
E. Millefiori paperweight, about 1850   81
F. Cameo vase by Thomas Webb & Sons, 1884   112
G. Fancy glass bowl by Stevens & Williams,
   about 1885   113
H. Decanter designed for James Powell & Sons, 1874   128
I. Pressed glass vase by John Derbyshire, about 1876   129

MONOCHROME PLATES

 1–13. Regency cut glass
14–27. Cut glass in the broad-fluted and other new styles of
       the 1820s to mid-fifties
28–31. Brilliant cut glass of the 1880s and 1890s
 32–3. Gilded glasses by Isaac Jacobs and William Absolon
34–48. 'Nailsea' and similar glasses of the early and middle
       parts of the century
   49. Davenport coated glass
 50–1. Glasses decorated with sulphides

52–5.   Mid-century stained, coloured and layered glasses

56–68. Opalines and other glasses with painted, gilded and printed decoration

69–72. Other fancy glasses of the middle of the century

73–82. Glasses engraved in early nineteenth-century styles

83–90. Engraved glasses of the 1840s, 1850s and 1860s

91–5.   Engraved glasses of the 1870s and 1880s

96–100. 'Rock crystal' engraving

101.   Glass with intaglio decoration

102–4. Glasses with etched decoration

105–9. Relief carving and cameo work

110–16. Uncoloured fancy glasses of the 1860s and later

117–18. Flower stands of the 1860s and 1870s

119–30. Fancy glasses of the 1880s and later

131–41. Glasses inspired by the Arts and Crafts movement

142–8. Early mould-blown and press-moulded glasses

149–66. Pressed-moulded glasses of the mid- and late-nineteenth century

Foreword

The history of English glass during the seventeenth and eighteenth centuries has been well served in literature. Rightly so, for this period saw the emergence of an English glass-material and an English style of decoration which were perfectly wedded to one another, and which by their combination revolutionized the glass industry of the world. This book therefore properly treats first of the 'Regency' heyday of cut glass. English cut glass, however, had its day, and the period which followed its decline has been less well studied than it deserves. A modern generation is perhaps too close to it in time to be sure of its own aesthetic discernment: but of the technical virtuosity and inventiveness of that era there can be no doubt whatever. There were giants in those days, and on these great men, bestriding their world and so sure of their own taste, it is perhaps unwise yet to sit in judgement.

In the meantime, it is well that their world should be accurately charted, and for this pioneer work Mr Wakefield is admirably qualified. To his preliminary survey undertaken for the Exhibition of Victorian and Edwardian Decorative Arts at the Victoria and Albert Museum in 1952 he has added many new landmarks, and an invaluable feature of his work is the number of securely dated and attributed pieces which he has incorporated, like triangulation-points, into the framework of his survey. However judgements may change in the future, this firm structure will endure. Nor is this mere dry map-reading, for Mr Wakefield brings to his task not only knowledge but an enthusiasm unaffected by current fashions.

R. J. CHARLESTON

11

Foreword to Second Edition

Mr Wakefield's book, first published in 1961, was a pioneering achievement in its field, and has been followed by a spate of writing on Victorian glass. It has therefore seemed right to re-issue the book to take account of the new facts and ideas which the intervening twenty years have thrown up. It has been brought up to date and supplemented with much new material, both in the text and in the illustrations.

R.J.C.

Acknowledgements

The author is greatly indebted to the owners of thirteen private collections and the administrators of twenty-six museums in this country and abroad, who have given permission for their specimens and photographs to be used for the illustrations in this book. Besides the Victoria and Albert Museum the author has drawn most heavily upon the Stourbridge Glass Collection, which has an especial significance in the study of nineteenth-century glassware. Previously known as the Stourbridge Borough Collection, it is now in the care of Dudley Metropolitan Borough and, with the Brierley Hill Glass Collection and other material, is housed in the Broadfield House Glass Museum, Kingswinford.

It would not be possible to detail all the many individuals who, directly and indirectly, have contributed information and ideas. Mention must, however, be made of the late John Northwood, jun., who was largely responsible for the formation of the Stourbridge Borough Collection and whose personal experience provided a direct link with the Stourbridge glassmen of the last century.

13

Introduction

Although a few relevant monographs have appeared in recent years, the nineteenth-century glassware of this country has been only slightly explored. This applies particularly to the Victorian part of the century, the arts of which are complex and have tended to provoke emotional rather than historical interest. In preparing this book the author has been conscious of the lack of secondary sources of information in many parts of the subject; and he has been equally conscious of the elements of chance which must be involved in conclusions based solely on one person's selection of original sources.

Not only is the subject complex because it is seen at short range; it is also complex because of the Victorian love of novelty for its own sake. In the eighteenth century the movement of fashion had been so general and uniform that it is normally possible to date a glass to a period of five or ten years without any knowledge at all of the identity of its manufacturer. Among nineteenth-century work it is difficult indeed to achieve an equivalent degree of certainty because of the strange interplay of ephemeral and long-lasting ideas. To take the instance of one glassmaking firm, Thomas Webb & Sons of Stourbridge have some twenty-five thousand items in their main series of patterns between 1837 and 1900; and yet from among these vast numbers some popular patterns, such as a three-lipped decanter of the early eighteen-seventies, have continued into common production today.

Another element in the complexity of nineteenth-century glass was an increasing tendency for different fashions to exist simultaneously at different levels of society. Without drawing any fine distinctions one can discern at least three main levels in the latter part of the century: an expensive style of cut and engraved crystal was intended for the opulent; a sparing furnace-decorated style of glassware was for the adherents of the Arts and Crafts movement; and an original and somewhat bizarre style of fancy glass, both handmade and pressed, was for the relatively unsophisticated. One might also add, in the fanciful glass toys and the cheap ruby flower stands, a style of glassware which still preserved some of the characteristics of peasant art.

INTRODUCTION

The glasswork of the nineteenth century must clearly be approached in a different spirit from that of previous periods. It is too near in time for us to be sure of our aesthetic judgements; on the other hand its nearness gives us the possibility of basing our knowledge securely on documentary examples. In compiling the illustrations for this book the aim has been to show examples which carry with them some evidence as to their origin, and this has in fact been possible with nearly all those relating to the last three-quarters of the century. Some of the subjects of the illustrations have been marked by the manufacturers or artists; some have been acquired as contemporary work by museums; some have been handed down in the families or firms of those who made them or had special knowledge of them. In illustrating the work of this period, when ideas were passed rapidly from glasshouse to glasshouse and from country to country, a modest documentary piece is clearly preferable to an attractive piece which can only be ascribed by inference. It may be added that wherever possible examples which are now in museums have been preferred, since they are more likely to remain available for reassessment than those in private hands.

Glassware shows a relatively attractive face during the nineteenth century; it is at least a face which the twentieth century can appreciate more readily than that of most other nineteenth-century arts. Of all materials glass lent itself least to excess of ornamentation and to stylistic eclecticism. Influences were borne upon the glassmaker from the most diverse sources, but the deliberate imitation of glassware from past ages was singularly rare. In spite of the appearance of mechanical means of pressing and blowing glass into moulds, the age-old processes of hand manipulation continued and flourished, and throughout the industrial revolution and its aftermath glassware can be found which expresses the craftsman's regard for the limitations and possibilities of the material. The possibilities did indeed expand during this century of conscious experimentation, and among the innumerable products of the British factories there are some at least which are undeniably beautiful and which for technical skill can scarcely be matched from earlier, or later, times.

Introduction to Second Edition

During the years which have elapsed since the appearance of the first edition a number of important works have been published dealing with various aspects of nineteenth-century glassware. In particular my erstwhile colleague Mrs Barbara Morris has dealt admirably, and in considerable detail, with the wares of the Victorian part of the century.

In preparing this second edition it has seemed reasonable to leave the original Introduction as before, although the complaint of the lack of secondary sources can no longer be sustained. The scope of the following chapters remains almost precisely the same as before, but many passages have been rewritten to introduce new facts and ideas or to effect corrections and changes of emphasis. A number of new illustrations have been added and some old ones removed, but as before preference has been given to the illustration of pieces which can be considered in some way documentary or are to be found in public collections.

The ownership of the objects illustrated has been updated where possible, but it should be said that the author has not necessarily confirmed the location of all the original material which was referred to in the first edition. The author's Acknowledgements have been slightly amended, although it remains impracticable to specify the innumerable sources of helpful information.

1

Cut Glass

At the opening of the nineteenth century the British glass factories were on the point of exerting their greatest influence on the world history of glass. Since the middle of the previous century they had been increasingly absorbed in the decorative possibilities of geometrical cutting on their soft lead glass; but it was in the early decades of the nineteenth century that they perfected their style of cutting in the manner in which it achieved its widest international popularity and in which it has survived to the present day as a well-respected tradition.

The British decorative arts of the early nineteenth century, and especially of the second and third decades, are usually described, somewhat loosely, as 'Regency'; and it will be convenient to use this term to describe the distinctive cut-glass style which matured in this period. It was a style of clear lead crystal in which the shape of vessels was subordinate to the decoration of them, and in which the decoration consisted mainly of deep mitre cuts in square patterns. Technically the Regency cut glass was an ultimate and logical development from the shallowly sliced glassware of the mid-eighteenth century. Stylistically its surface brilliance and its squat solidity of form expressed as nearly as could be in glassware the sense of dignity and ostentation which was characteristic of all the arts of the British Regency and of the continental Empire styles.

Since the middle of the nineteenth century writers on decorative art subjects have often condemned the cutting of glass on theoretical grounds, and for this reason the historical significance of Regency glass has been largely overlooked. Judged by the extent of its dissemination and the continuing strength of its influence, glass in this style can be compared with the sixteenth-century furnace-manipulated glass of Venice or the Central European engraved glass of the seventeenth and eighteenth centuries. The successful imitation of British cut glass was a main cause of the development of the great French and Belgian factories in the first half of the nineteenth century. The style was widely followed in the United States of America. The inability of the Venetian glasshouses to imitate it in their soda-lime glass was a main cause of the eclipse of Venice as a glassmaking centre in the early part of the century. Even in Central Europe the Regency style of cut glass could only be partially resisted, in spite of the appearance of the 'Biedermeier' coloured glasses in the eighteen-twenties and thirties.

It is a curious paradox that this peak in the influence of British glassmaking should have coincided with the period of the Glass Excise, whereby successive governments between 1745 and 1845 sought to obtain revenue from an elaborately organized tax on the output of the glass factories. It is perhaps even more curious that although the excise was levied by weight of glass the achievement of the British glassmakers was in a style of glassware which necessitated the making of vessels of great thickness. The excise seems to have had the effect of concentrating the main effort of the British glassmakers upon the one current style of clear glass with cut decoration. This concentration may well have been beneficial, at least until the eighteen-twenties; and in general we may suspect that the evidence which is usually adduced on the effects of the excise, coming chiefly from established manufacturers, is highly partisan and presents an exaggerated picture of its evils.

The paradox has been generally explained in the past by an assumption that a large part of the British decorative glassware of the period was made in Ireland, and hence the period of British glass history between about 1780 and 1825 has been often referred to as the 'Anglo-Irish' period. During that time manufacturers of fine glassware in Ireland were free from the excise and also from previous export restrictions. In consequence a part of the British glass industry was transplanted to Ireland in spite of the increased cost of raw materials, and factories were established in such centres as Waterford, Cork, Dublin and Belfast. These factories came to be particularly associated with the trade across the Atlantic, and Irish records show that by far the greater part of the exported Irish glass went in that direction.[1] The subsequent decline of the Irish industry in the late twenties and thirties was probably due mainly to changes in the transatlantic markets, although the imposition of the excise duty in Ireland in 1825 must also have been a contributory factor. Waterford, the last of the important early Irish factories, closed in 1851, in the very year when its products were on display at the Great Exhibition in London.

Through close study it may be possible to isolate certain forms and motifs which received especial emphasis in the Irish factories or which in some instances are peculiar to them, but these scarcely seem to constitute a basis for stylistic differentiation.[2] From the number of factories involved it is clear that the output of the Irish factories can never have been very great compared with that of the factories in the remainder of the United Kingdom. The Irish factories were never more than about ten in number; while in Britain the number of factories concerned with decorative glass was considerably greater. Some indication of the

[1] M. S. Dudley Westropp, *Irish Glass*, revised edn., Dublin (1978), pp. 145–57.
[2] Phelps Warren has published many documented Irish pieces in his *Irish Glass*, 2nd edn., London (1981).

1. Cut-glass DISH with cover. Ht. 15 cm (5.9 in). Early nineteenth century. *Victoria and Albert Museum. See page 22*

2. Cut-glass DISH with cover, oval section. Ht. 17.2 cm (6.75 in). Early nineteenth century. *Victoria and Albert Museum. See page 22*

relative output of lead glass (or flint glass as it was usually called) is given by the excise statistics, although it should be remembered that this heading of tax covered all uses of the material and included all the legal production of such small containers as medicine bottles and ink wells. From these statistics, quoted by the Excise Commissioners of Inquiry in 1835, it can be seen that when the excise was introduced in Ireland in the middle twenties it was producing under the heading of flint glass about £20,000 a year, compared with rather more than £20,000 in Scotland and more than £150,000 in England. The Irish industry may not have been at its peak in 1825, but about ten flint glasshouses were operating and the complaints collected by the Excise Commissioners all seem to imply that the industry was in a relatively flourishing state when the excise was first levied.[3] The tendency to describe cut glass indiscriminately as 'Irish', or even as 'Waterford', is probably due largely to accidental factors in the history of research. Certainly the history of the Irish factories in the early nineteenth century is well known; whereas historians dealing with the wider field of British glass have tended to avoid the complicated research, which is still awaited, into the history of the British factories of the period.

The characteristic decoration of Regency glass consisted of mitre cutting, that is, V-section grooves cut into the surface of the glass. By far the greater part of the cutting was in straight lines, and the main motifs were formed by parallel cuttings intersecting at ninety or forty-five degrees. In its simplest form the intersection of cuttings at ninety degrees produced a field of plain 'diamonds', which was in effect a series of small pyramids (Plates 3, 6, 10). Among the many possible variants of this sort of decoration, the fields of complicated 'strawberry diamonds' came to be one of the most popular. In this pattern the spacing of mitre cuts in two directions produced a series of rectangular surfaces which were themselves covered by a criss-cross of tiny cut lines (Plates 8, 11, 12). Other motifs involved the use of radiating cuts. The base of a vessel would usually be 'star-cut', and its rim might be decorated with 'fan-cutting' on each of a series of semi-circular protrusions (Plate 5).

The shapes used for Regency cut glass can in general be distinguished from their late eighteenth-century precursors by a certain formal heaviness which seems to concentrate attention on the cut decoration; and it is noticeable that the decoration is more often arranged horizontally than vertically (Plates 1, 2). The decanters of the period were mostly barrel-shaped (Plates 3, 9), often with a number of rings in relief round their necks and usually with 'mushroom' stoppers. Wineglasses or 'rummers' were set low on short stems, often with disc-shaped knops. Their bowls were either convex or straight sided, and besides the short bucket shapes the latter included tall 'flute' glasses (Plates 7, 8, 73, 74).

[3] *Thirteenth Report of the Commissioners of Inquiry into the Excise Establishment, etc. (Glass)*, London (1835).

3. Cut-glass DECANTER with 'mushroom' stopper. Ht. 24.2 cm (9.5 in). About
1820. *Victoria and Albert Museum. See page 22*

4. Two cut-glass JUGS. Hts. 8.3 cm (3.25 in) and 14.9 cm (5.9 in). About 1815. *Victoria and Albert Museum. See page 29*

5. Oval cut-glass DISH. Length 21.9 cm (8.6 in). About 1820. *Victoria and Albert Museum. See page 22*

---

6. (*facing, above*) WINE COOLER with cover and stand, decorated mainly with plain diamond and prism cutting. Ht. 37.5 cm (14.75 in). About 1815. *Victoria and Albert Museum. See pages 22, 29*

7. (*facing, below left*) 'Flute' WINEGLASS with cut decoration. Ht. 14.6 cm (5.75 in). Early nineteenth century. *Victoria and Albert Museum. See page 22*

8. (*facing, below right*) GLASS with cut and engraved decoration. Ht. 12.1 cm (4.75 in). Used at a banquet given for George IV in Edinburgh in 1822. *Royal Scottish Museum. See page 22*

9. Cut-glass DECANTER. Ht. 28 cm (11 in). Cut by William & Thomas Powell of Temple Gate, Bristol, on glass made by the firm of Badger at the Phoenix glassworks, DUDLEY, about 1830. *City Art Gallery, Bristol. See page 22*

10. Cut-glass TUMBLER. Ht. 12.1 cm (4.75 in). Made by the firm of Henry Ricketts at the Phoenix glassworks, Temple Gate, BRISTOL, probably about 1825. *City Art Gallery, Bristol.* See page 22

11. Cut-glass TODDY LIFTER, engraved with the letter 'S' for Augustus Frederick, Duke of Sussex (1801–43). Length 21.3 cm (8.4 in). Probably made in the 1820s. *Victoria and Albert Museum. See page 22*

12. BOWL, cut with strawberry diamonds. Ht. 8.9 cm (3.5 in). Probably made in the 1820s. *Victoria and Albert Museum. See page 22*

13. Cut-glass DECANTER and GLASSES, with engraved insignia of the Prince of Wales. Ht. of decanter 34.9 cm (13.75 in). From a royal service, second decade of the nineteenth century. *Victoria and Albert Museum. See page 29*

Perhaps because the sharp angles of intersecting mitre cutting were never considered very suitable for drinking glasses, their decoration was usually in the form of flat vertical facets towards the lower part of the bowl. Jugs were proportionately numerous in the output of the period, but such vessels had only recently become popular in glassware and the Regency versions of them seem to have the awkwardness which derives from imitating pottery shapes (Plate 4). The more ambitious work included swirling pillar cutting, protruding gadroon-like motifs and elaborately shaped feet (Plates 6, 13).

The Regency style of cutting was the style which exerted the greatest international influence and which may be regarded as the classical standard of British glass cutting. Its survival was not, however, continuous at the highest level of fashion. In the new designs of the years about 1825–30 a change of emphasis can be seen from horizontal to vertical motifs, and from mitre cutting to the predominant use again of flat cutting or surface slicing. An object which in the second decade of the century might have been decorated with a horizontal band of diamonds would in the fourth decade be decorated characteristically with a vertical arrangement of broad 'flutes', usually flat or 'pillared' (i.e. convex in section) (Plates 18, 19). The essentials of this broad-fluted style can be seen in the pattern drawings of about 1830 which belonged to Samuel Miller, the foreman cutter at the Waterford glassworks in Ireland.[4] It has been stated that the style emanated from the cutting shops of Birmingham,[5] and certain examples acquired by the Paris Conservatoire National des Arts et Métiers from Birmingham about 1820 may be regarded as early examples in this development. These included a decanter and jug with strongly vertical motifs, together with some forward-looking wineglasses with continuous fluting from the bowl into the stem (Plates 14–16). Also about 1820 markedly vertical arrangements of fine diamond panels alternating with 'pillared' flutes were being used by the London firm of Pellatt & Green on glasses enclosing sulphides (Plate 50. See page 57); such treatment was often used on the Continent, and is further illustrated here in a standing bowl from the Davenport factory at Longport (Plate 17). In its widest sense the broad-fluted style was an international style with reminiscences of the early eighteenth century, and it was especially associated with the Biedermeier glass of Central Europe. The tendency to concentrate on the vertical arrangement of motifs, and in particular on the cutting of broad vertical flutes, was probably connected with the appearance about the same time of straight-sided and angular shapes. A surface can be decorated most easily with vertical flutes if it is curved in only one direction. The most obvious instance of this change of shape was that of the decanters, which are seen to change with the style of cutting from the barrel shape to the more or less vertically sided cylindrical shape (Plate 18); it may be

---

[4] M. S. Dudley Westropp, *Irish Glass*, revised edn., Dublin (1978), p. 56, etc.
[5] *Pottery Gazette*, 1883, p. 269; 1884, p. 73; and 1889, p. 238.

14, 15. Cut-glass DECANTER and JUG. Hts. 25.5 cm (10 in) and 18 cm (7.1 in). Acquired in Birmingham about 1820. *Photograph by the Musée des Techniques, Conservatoire National des Arts et Métiers, Paris. See page 29*

16. WINEGLASSES with cut decoration. Hts. 13.5 cm (5.3 in) and 14.5 cm
(5.75 in). Acquired in Birmingham about 1820. *Photograph by the Musée des
Techniques, Conservatoire National des Arts et Métiers, Paris. See page 29*

17. Cut-glass standing BOWL. Diam. 24.8 cm (9.75 in). Made by the Davenport
firm at Longport, STOKE-ON-TRENT, probably about 1820. *Stoke-on-Trent
City Museum and Art Gallery, Hanley. See page 29*

18. DECANTER with pillar cutting.
    Ht. 28 cm (11 in). Probably made in
    the 1830s. *Stourbridge Glass Collection.*
    See page 29

19. Cut-glass DISH with cover and stand.
    Ht. 15.2 cm (6 in). Probably made in
    the 1830s. *Stourbridge Glass Collection.*
    See page 29

noticed that many of the straight-tapering flute wineglasses belong also to this phase of straight-sided shapes. The cylindrical decanter, and the broad-fluted style of cutting that went with it, may be considered the basic type of the thirties and early forties. Inevitably, however, there was some degree of elaboration in all the more ambitious work, so that the flutes would assume multiple profiles and would often alternate with panels of complicated mitre cutting. Along with this came a strong fashion for arched patterns, which were often complex in detail but were nevertheless arranged with markedly vertical emphasis (Plates 20, 21).

An illustration of the styles in use in the later thirties is provided by a price list issued by the firm of Apsley Pellatt. An abridged version of the list, illustrated on Plate 22, was issued as an advertisement in publications, including the serial edition of Charles Dickens' *Nicholas Nickleby* from November 1838.[6] This shows the influence of the broad-fluted style of decoration at this time. It shows also in the globular 'water bottles' another thread in the history of British glass leading towards the use of curvilinear shapes. The broad-fluted work was related to Regency glass, and with its tendency towards angular profiles it can in effect be considered as a later manifestation of the international Empire style. The British makers of silverwork and porcelain, on the other hand, had been reacting directly against the heavy angularity of Empire work since the second decade of the century, and were working mainly in a revived version of the eighteenth-century rococo style. Glassmakers were slow to follow because neither the forms nor the elaborately curved and asymmetrical motifs of the revived rococo could be appropriately rendered in cut glass; but during the thirties and early forties a feeling for curving shapes and motifs was developing as a subsidiary element in the glassware of the period. Water-carafes and decanters were appearing with globular bodies, and champagne glasses with hemispherical bowls were being acclaimed as a novelty.[7] Wineglasses with bell-shaped or ogee-curved profiles were also becoming increasingly common through the thirties and forties (Plates 84, 85, 87(a)). Cut decoration often consisted of plain facets running through from the stem to the bowl and the facets might arise from a characteristic 'drop' stem (Plate 52). The globular decanters and similar vessels were often cut with rows of shallow hollows or 'printies' (Plate 27). Sometimes heavy mitre cutting was used (Colour Plate B); but the most appropriate decoration for strongly curving shapes was by engraving, and the period of their most extended use was to coincide with the eclipse of heavy cutting in the sixties and seventies.

In 1845, after a long agitation, the Glass Excise was removed. One of the effects of this event was to revive interest in deep mitre-cut glass without any inhibitions as to the thickness of the glass or the depth of the cutting (Plate 24). For some time

[6] A full list was illustrated by the present author in R. J. Charleston etc., *Studies in Glass History and Design*, Sheffield (1968), where however the approximate date was wrongly identified as 1842, as also in the author's article in *Antiques*, January 1965.

[7] W. A. Thorpe, *History of English and Irish Glass*, London and Boston (1929), vol. I, p. 314.

20. DECANTER, cut with arch pillars. Ht. 30.5 cm (12 in). About 1840–5. *Stourbridge Glass Collection. See page 33*

21. Cut-glass DECANTER with arch decoration. Ht. 33 cm (13 in). About 1840–5. *Stourbridge Glass Collection. See page 33*

APSLEY PELLATT'S
ABRIDGED LIST OF
Net Cash Prices for the best Flint Glass Ware.

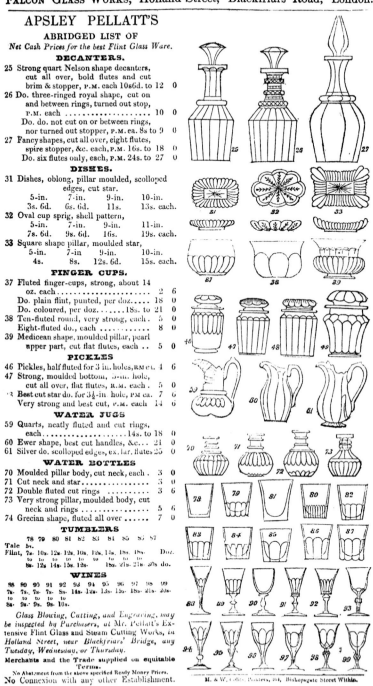

DECANTERS.

25 Strong quart Nelson shape decanters, cut all over, bold flutes and cut brim & stopper, P.M. each 10s6d. to 12 0

26 Do. three-ringed royal shape, cut on and between rings, turned out stop, P.M. each 10 0
Do. do. not cut on or between rings, nor turned out stopper, P.M. ea. 8s to 9 0

27 Fancy shapes, cut all over, eight flutes, spire stopper, &c. each, P.M. 16s. to 18 0
Do. six flutes only, each, P.M. 24s. to 27 0

DISHES.

31 Dishes, oblong, pillar moulded, scolloped edges, cut star.

| 5-in. | 7-in. | 9-in. | 10-in. |
| 3s. 6d. | 6s. 6d. | 11s. | 13s. each. |

32 Oval cup sprig, shell pattern,

| 5-in. | 7-in. | 9-in. | 11-in. |
| 7s. 6d. | 9s. 6d. | 16s. | 19s. each. |

33 Square shape pillar, moulded star,

| 5-in. | 7-in | 9-in. | 10-in. |
| 4s. | 8s. | 12s. 6d. | 15s. each. |

FINGER CUPS.

37 Fluted finger-cups, strong, about 14 oz. each 2 6
Do. plain flint, punted, per doz..... 18 0
Do. coloured, per doz........18s. to 21 0

38 Ten-fluted round, very strong, each . 5 0
Eight-fluted do., each 8 0

39 Medicean shape, moulded pillar, pearl upper part, cut flat flutes, each .. 5 0

PICKLES

46 Pickles, half fluted for 3 in. holes, RM ea. 4 6

47 Strong, moulded bottom, 3-in. hole, cut all over, flat flutes, R.M. each . 5 0
48 Best cut star do. for 3½-in hole, PM ea. 7 6
Very strong and best cut, P.M. each 14 6

WATER JUGS

59 Quarts, neatly fluted and cut rings, each....................14s. to 18 0
60 Ewer shape, best cut handles, &c... 21 0
61 Silver do. scolloped edges, ex. lar. flutes 25 0

WATER BOTTLES

70 Moulded pillar body, cut neck, each . 3 0
71 Cut neck and star................ 3 0
72 Double fluted cut rings 3 6
73 Very strong pillar, moulded body, cut neck and rings 5 6
74 Grecian shape, fluted all over 7 0

TUMBLERS

	78	79	80	81	82	83	84	85	86	87	
Tale 5s.											
Flint,	7s.	10s.	12s.	12s.	10s.	12s.	14s.	18s.	18s.		Doz.
	to	to	to	to	to	to	to	to	to		
	8s.	12s.	14s.	15s.	12s.	16s.	21s.	21s.	30s.		do.

WINES

	88	89	90	91	92	93	94	95	96	97	98	99
	7s.	7s.	7s.	7s.	8s.	14s.	12s.	13s.	15s.	18s.	21s.	20s.
	to	to	to	to	to							
	8s.	9s.	9s.	9s.	10s.							

Glass Blowing, Cutting, and Engraving, may be inspected by Purchasers, at Mr. Pellatt's Extensive Flint Glass and Steam Cutting Works, in Holland Street, near Blackfriars' Bridge, any Tuesday, Wednesday, or Thursday.

Merchants and the **Trade** supplied on **equitable Terms.**

No Abatement from the above specified Ready Money Prices.

No Connexion with any other Establishment.

M. & W. Collis, Printers, 104, Bishopsgate Street Within.

22. Abridged PRICE LIST of the firm of Apsley Pellatt, issued as an advertisement in publications from 1838. Photograph taken from the serial edition of Charles Dickens' *Nicholas Nickleby*, Part VIII, November 1838. *The Dickens House, London. See page 33*

the motifs of mitre cutting, when used, had tended to be large and prominent (Plate 23), and this became now a marked feature of the mid-century work (Plate 25). Increasing use was also made of difficult curvilinear motifs, and the shapes of the vessels were freer and more variable than they had ever been before. The most extravagant work was shown at the Great Exhibition of 1851 and is well illustrated in contemporary engravings of the exhibition displays. It is nevertheless fortunate that some of the pieces which were shown, or are reasonably presumed to have been shown, by the leading Stourbridge firm of W. H., B. & J. Richardson have survived to the present day (Plates 25, 26). These are deeply and elaborately cut, but their cut patterns are pleasingly integrated with their shapes, and they are by no means the 'prickly monstrosities' that such pieces appear to be when seen through the medium of inaccurately drawn nineteenth-century engravings. It should be mentioned here that the centrepiece of the exhibition was an enormous fountain of cut glass ingeniously constructed by the Birmingham firm of F. & C. Osler, which over a long period made a speciality of producing outsize glass objects for exhibitions and for eastern potentates.

The 1851 exhibition was followed by a long period during which cut glassware was relatively disregarded. Throughout the later fifties, sixties and seventies the crystal glassware most highly thought of was that decorated by engraving, and the most favoured shapes were the curvilinear ones which are suited to that form of decoration. Naturally cut glass was still made, and in considerable quantities, both for this country and abroad; but it is clear from makers' pattern books that little original thought was being given to cut-glass patterns during these decades, and new designs tended to be comparatively unassuming. The displays at international exhibitions tended to exaggerate the prevailing taste; but there is little doubt from the accounts of the British glass at the International Exhibition of 1862 in London and the Universal Exhibitions of 1867 and 1878 in Paris that the trend of fashion in this period was fully against cutting as a method of decoration.

This reaction against cut glass was no doubt due partly to the appearance of effective pressed glass imitations.[8] By the middle of the century the intellectual revolt against the cutting of glass was also under way. John Ruskin in the second volume of his *Stones of Venice*, published in 1853, declared in a strongly worded passage that 'all cut glass is barbaric'. Sentiments of this sort had been expressed before, although more mildly, by writers in the *Art Union*[9] and the *Journal of Design and Manufactures*,[10] and by Richard Redgrave in his report on design at the 1851 exhibition.[11] Such views would not necessarily work in favour of glass engraving, which is equally independent of the furnace, but they may well have

[8] E. M. Elville, *Apollo Annual*, London (1951), p. 57.
[9] 1848, p. 126.
[10] Vol. III, 1850, pp. 16 et seq. and 82.
[11] *Reports by the Juries* (1851 exhibition, single volume edition), p. 735.

23. Cut-glass EPERGNE. Ht. 100.3 cm (39.5 in). Said to have been decorated by Richard Hunter, foreman glasscutter at the glassworks of John Ford, EDINBURGH, and completed in 1840. *Huntly House Museum, Edinburgh.*
See pages 37, 117

24. Cut-glass DECANTER. Ht. 38.1 cm (15 in). About 1850. *Stourbridge Glass Collection. See page 33*

25. Cut-glass DECANTER. Ht. 37.5 cm (14.75 in). Made by W. H., B. and J. Richardson, STOURBRIDGE, and said to have been shown at the 1851 exhibition. *Mr W. Worrall (a descendant of the Richardson family). Victoria and Albert Museum photograph.* See page 37

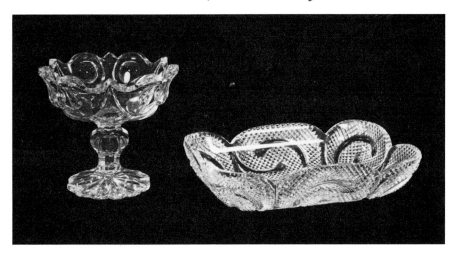

26. Cut-glass COMPORT and DISH.
Hts. 13.6 cm (5.4 in) and
5.4 cm (2.1 in). Both made by
W. H., B. & J. Richardson,
STOURBRIDGE, and said to
have been shown in the 1851
exhibition. *Stourbridge Glass
Collection and Mr W. Worrall (a
descendant of the Richardson family).
Victoria and Albert Museum
photograph. See page 37*

27. Cut-glass DECANTER.
Ht. 31 cm (12.25 in). Made by
Apsley Pellatt, LONDON, 1851.
*Photograph by the Musée des
Techniques, Conservatoire National
des Arts et Métiers, Paris.
See page 33*

41

28. Cut-glass DECANTER. Ht. 35.6 cm (14 in). Made by Stevens & Williams, BRIERLEY HILL. Designed in 1887. *In the possession of the makers (Victoria and Albert Museum photograph).* See page 45

29. Cut-glass CLARET JUG, engraved with the arms of the King of Italy.
Ht. 36.3 cm (14.25 in). Made by F. & C. Osler, BIRMINGHAM, about 1893.
*Formerly in the possession of Mr Peter A. G. Osler. Victoria and Albert Museum
photograph. See page 45*

30. Cut-glass BASKET. Ht. 17.5 cm (6.9 in). Made by Stevens & Williams, BRIERLEY HILL, about 1880. *In the possession of the makers. See page 45*

31. Cut-glass BOWL. Diam. 41.9 cm (16.5 in). Decorated by E. Hammond at Stevens & Williams, BRIERLEY HILL, about 1895. *In the possession of the makers. See page 45*

contributed to the eclipse of cut glass. It is important to notice, however, that by this time fashions in glass were largely international. In the other important glassmaking centres which had established a trade in the British style of cut glass, in Central Europe, France and the United States of America, this was equally a period in which cut decoration was being given comparatively little attention.

The reaction came with the eighties and nineties, when cut glass was again to the fore; and its return to favour was certainly an international movement. In America the revival has been referred to as the Brilliant period of cut glass (a term which may reasonably be extended to the equivalent phase in Britain and elsewhere), and it is particularly associated with the great Libbey Glass Company which was eventually established at Toledo, Ohio. In Sweden, the revival in the nineties coincided with the industrial development which led that country to become for the first time a considerable exporter of glassware. In the surviving pattern books of British manufacturers a great number of new designs can be seen from the eighties and nineties in which cutting is carried to the farthest extremity of elaboration. The characteristic feature of the work itself was the exact mathematical precision to which the cutters aspired. Usually composed of bold groupings of relatively small elements, the decoration gave an effect of great richness (Plates 28, 31). Technical improvements led to greater control of the cutting and made it possible to produce on a commercial scale such seemingly difficult subjects as cut-glass baskets (Plate 30). A square-section spirit decanter decorated all over with diamond mitre cutting and with a lapidary stopper, was typical of the period, and a number of these were often ranged together on a lockable 'spirit stand' or 'tantalus'. Objects such as wine decanters, claret jugs and flower vases appeared in a wide variety of profiles, often tall and slim and usually on spreading feet (Plates 28, 29). Cut glass retained a conservative air — it was referred to by manufacturers as the 'old legitimate trade'[12] — but inevitably it reflected in the variety of its shapes something of the freedom which was characteristic of the fancy coloured glassware of the same period.

The period of the Brilliant cut glass was one of great activity by the British glass firms in the designing and making of many different sorts of glassware; but it was during these decades that cut glass came to be regarded again as the standard of middle and upper-class elegance. An intellectual distaste for it continued, but the wider prejudices generated by pressed-glass imitations had clearly been set aside as cut glass became more than ever the symbol of social and material success.

[12] *Pottery Gazette*, 1889, p. 791.

2

Earlier Coloured Glass and Novelties

In spite of great technical advances in the methods of colouring glass, the use of coloured glass was by no means a consistent feature of nineteenth-century glassmaking. At both the popular and more sophisticated levels of production coloured glassware was largely subject to changes of fashion; and this applied not merely to the prevalence of colour from one decade to another, but also to the manner in which it was used. As in the case of cut glass, two main periods of activity in the use of coloured glasses were divided by a period of comparative inactivity around the sixties. This chapter is concerned with the various uses of coloured glass and other novelties up to the time of the 1851 exhibition; a later chapter will deal with the coloured fancy glasses of the later part of the century.

The second half of the eighteenth century had seen in Britain the development of the deeply coloured glasses and the painted opaque-white glasses which are known generically as 'Bristol' glass. The last decade or so of the century also saw the beginning of the coloured 'Nailsea' ware, which may be considered as decorated glassware at the most popular level. At the beginning of the nineteenth century some of the 'Bristol' wares were still being made. Although it is presumed that much of the work of this sort was made elsewhere than at Bristol, it was at this town that Isaac Jacobs announced in 1805 his 'Non-such Flint Glass Manufactory' and in the following year was advertising the dessert set which he 'had the honour of sending to her Majesty in burnished Gold upon Royal purple colored Glass'.[1] It is fortunate that some of Jacobs' wares can be identified by the signature which he inscribed on them (Plate 32). About the same time William Absolon, the independent painter of Yarmouth, was decorating opaque white and coloured glasses as well as uncoloured glasses and ceramic objects (Plate 33). In general, however, fashionable glasses in coloured or opaque-white material were somewhat unusual in the early decades of the century when interest was concentrated largely on clear uncoloured glassware.

[1] A. C. Powell, *Trans. Bristol and Gloucestershire Archaeological Society*, vol. XLVII (1925), p. 239.

32. FINGER BOWL, and PLATE or STAND, both of blue glass with gilded decoration. Diam. of plate 20.3 cm (8 in). Made by Isaac Jacobs, BRISTOL (the stand is marked), about 1805–10. *City Art Gallery, Bristol. See page 46*

33. MUG of opaque white glass, with gilded decoration. Ht. 12 cm (4.75 in). Signed by William Absolon of Yarmouth. Early nineteenth century. *Victoria and Albert Museum. See page 46*

The history of 'Nailsea' glass was very different. The name is used for a variety of wares which have an unsophisticated 'peasant-art' appearance. Some of these were made in darkly coloured bottle glass, others in more refined glasses, usually of the greenish window-glass type. They were decorated by opaque-white or coloured glass splashed or applied to the surface in trailed-on stripes, and they might be further decorated with spiral trailing in clear glass or with pincered work. Most of the larger 'Nailsea' objects and those intended for practical table use, such as jugs, decanter-bottles and mugs, were made of the unrefined bottle glass and were decorated with splashing in white or in several colours together, or else were decorated with white stripes which were often looped to give a waved effect (Plates 34–7). On the other hand most of the examples in clearer refined glasses are pocket flasks or decorative objects such as fancy rolling pins and imitative fire bellows (Plates 38–42). Here the decoration was nearly always striped and looped, and it was often carried out in two colours, white and ruby. The body material of this group might consist, alternatively, of opaque white glass; and this was particularly so in the case of the flasks, which might be made either singly or joined together in pairs as 'gimmel flasks'.

There is little doubt that the first group of 'Nailsea' glasses, the practical tableware made in bottle glass, was an offshoot of the bottle-making industry, and its development in this milieu must have been connected with the fact that the Glass Excise fell least heavily on unrefined bottle glass. It belongs roughly to the last two decades of the eighteenth century and the first three of the nineteenth century, and may be regarded as the first truly cheap and popular decorative glass made in Britain. Perhaps because the material was strikingly different from clear lead glass, its development bore little relation to the fashionable cut glass of the time. It may be presumed that it lost favour about the middle of the thirties, when its popular market was swept by pressed glass and the humblest householders found that they could afford to use clear-glass ware which was a fair imitation of expensive cut glass. The second group of 'Nailsea' glasses, more ornamental in nature, may be considered a parallel and somewhat later development. This group was less affected by the competition of pressed glass, and indeed most of the examples may well be subsequent to the removal of the excise in 1845.

The ware has derived its name from association with the factory at Nailsea, near Bristol, which made window glass and had bottle-glass connections. From the considerable quantities which have survived we may presume that it was widely made elsewhere in the bottle-glass and window-glass factories and even, later, in those making clear lead glass, but because it must usually have been a sideline, there is little documentary evidence of its production. Two of the very few dated examples are illustrated here. Both are of bottle glass, one from Ireland, the other from Scotland, bearing the dates 1809 and 1827 (Plates 35, 36). One typical bottle-glass jug with coloured splashing is believed to have been made in the Donnington Wood glasshouses in Shropshire (otherwise known as

34. JUG of unrefined amber-green glass
with white striped decoration.
Ht. 17.8 cm (7 in). Probably early
nineteenth century. *Victoria and Albert
Museum. See page 48*

35. FLASK of unrefined green glass, with
white striped decoration and seal dated
1809. Ht. 19.1 cm (7.5 in). *National
Museum of Ireland, Dublin. See page 48*

36. DECANTER-BOTTLE of unrefined amber-coloured glass with white splashing and pincered decoration. Ht. 29.5 cm (11.6 in). The inscription on the seal includes the date 1827 and probably implies that the bottle was made in SCOTLAND. *Victoria and Albert Museum. See page 48*

37. JUG of unrefined green glass splashed with coloured glasses. Ht. 24.2 cm (9.5 in). Believed to have been made in the DONNINGTON WOOD (otherwise known as Wrockwardine Wood) glasshouses, Shropshire. Early nineteenth century. *Victoria and Albert Museum. See pages 48, 53*

38. (*right*) FLASK of clear glass with looped white and ruby striped decoration covered by an outer trailing of clear glass. Ht. 18.4 cm (7.25 in). Probably made in the second quarter of the nineteenth century. *Victoria and Albert Museum. See page 48*

39. (*below*) FLASK with white and ruby striped decoration. Ht. 21 cm (8.25 in). Said to have been made by a glassblower named Joseph Lane at the Cockhedge glassworks, WARRINGTON, in 1857. *Museum and Art Gallery, Warrington. See pages 48, 53*

40. (*bottom*) ROLLING PIN of clear glass with looped white and ruby stripes. Length 33.7 cm (13.25 in). Probably made in the second quarter of the nineteenth century. *Victoria and Albert Museum. See page 48*

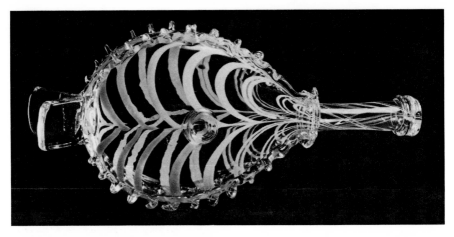

41. BELLOWS FLASK of clear glass with white striped and pincered decoration. Length 20.3 cm (8 in). Probably made in the second quarter of the nineteenth century. *Victoria and Albert Museum.* *See page 48*

42. BELLOWS ORNAMENT with white and ruby striped decoration. Ht. 38.1 cm (15 in). Said to have been made at the Bank Quay glassworks, WARRINGTON, about 1840. *Museum and Art Gallery, Warrington.* *See pages 48, 53*

the Wrockwardine Wood glasshouses) (Plate 37). A number of clear-glass pieces are known to have been made in glasshouses in Warrington (Plates 39, 42). In Scotland the term 'Alloa' is often used in the same context as 'Nailsea', and although there seems to be little direct evidence it can be said that the Alloa glasshouse was a likely producer of these wares.

Many other simple wares akin to 'Nailsea' were made in the first half of the century. Some were in greenish unrefined glass (Plate 43(b)). Others were made in deliberately coloured or opaque white material, in a style which seems to be associated with the Newcastle upon Tyne area (Plates 43(a), 44). Some of these wares bore popular inscriptions or painted decorations which were unfired and have therefore rarely survived unimpaired. In the same category were many glass rolling pins, and the fancy products of the glassmakers' virtuosity known as 'friggers'. The rolling pins are reputed to have been made for sailors to present to their wives and sweethearts, and many of them, made of blue or opaque-white glass, have inscriptions appropriate to this purpose (Plate 45). The friggers are elaborately wrought representations in glass of objects such as tobacco pipes and walking sticks for which glass was a surprising or unusual material (Plates 46–8). Many of the fancy tobacco pipes, as well as rolling pins, bear a striped decoration in opaque-white and coloured glasses which associates them directly with the 'Nailsea' tradition. It is often difficult to distinguish between the friggers, which can be considered as individual objects of virtuosity and amuse-ment, and similar fanciful glass toys made entirely for commercial purposes. No doubt friggers were made throughout the century; but interest in them was greatly revived towards the end of the century when small factories or workshops were producing ruby pipes, bells and walking sticks in considerable quantities.

Mention may be made here of a novelty of the early years of the century which was designed for a more sophisticated market. In 1806 John Davenport (whose firm made glass as well as pottery at Longport in Staffordshire) patented 'A New Method of Ornamenting of all Kinds of Glass in Imitation of Engraving or Etching, by Means of which Borders, Cyphers, Coats-of-Arms, Drawings, and the Most Elaborate Designs may be Executed in a Stile of Elegance'. His method was to lay on to the surface of a glass a thin coating of a powdered glass paste. A pattern was then formed by scraping off the coating with a pointed tool, after which the remains of the coating was lightly fired into the surface. This patent apparently refers to a group of glasses which have the word 'Patent' inscribed on their bases, and which are decorated with patterns varying from heraldic insignia to elaborate sporting scenes with figures in costume of about the first decade of the century (Plate 49). Although it was at one time assumed that this decoration was achieved by acid etching,[2] it has proved possible to remove

---

[2] G. E. Pazaurek, *Gläser der Empire- und Biedermeierzeit*, Leipzig (1923), p. 346; Arthur Churchill Ltd (London), *Glass Notes, No. 6* (1946), p. 10.

43. Two JUGS: (a) purple glass with the remains of an unfired gilded inscription 'Be canny with the Cream', (b) unrefined green glass with trailed decoration. Hts. 11.1 cm (4.4 in) and 14 cm (5.5 in). Probably of the early nineteenth century. *Victoria and Albert Museum. See page 53*

44. SUGAR BASIN of opaque white glass with unfired painted decoration. Ht. 11.1 cm (4.4 in). Probably made in the second quarter of the nineteenth century. *Kirklees Museums Service (Tolson Memorial Museum, Huddersfield). See page 53*

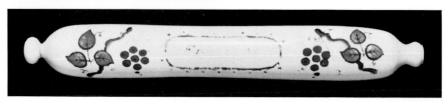

45. ROLLING PIN of opaque white glass, with unfired painted decoration including the remains of an inscription 'Forget me not'. Length 34.9 cm (13.75 in). First half of the nineteenth century. *Victoria and Albert Museum. See page 53*

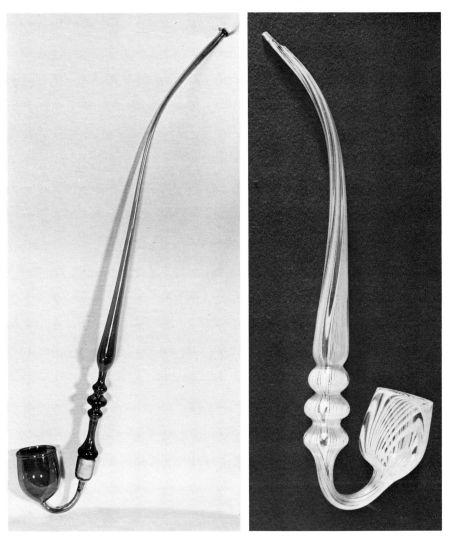

46. (*left*) Ruby PIPE. Length 92.7 cm (36.5 in). Said to have been made about 1840, probably at the Orford Lane glassworks, WARRINGTON. *Museum and Art Gallery, Warrington. See page 53*

47. (*right*) Glass PIPE, with white striped decoration. Length 36.8 cm (14.5 in). Said to have been made at the Sowerby factory, GATESHEAD, about 1860. *Tyne and Wear County Council Museums (Laing Art Gallery, Newcastle upon Tyne). See page 53*

48. Glass WALKING STICKS: (a) green glass, twisted, (b) clear glass containing ruby and white canes. Lengths 88.9 cm (35 in) and 73.7 cm (29 in). Said to have been made in WARRINGTON, at the Orford Lane glassworks about 1840 and at the Cockhedge glassworks about 1857. *Museum and Art Gallery, Warrington. See page 53*

fragments from the grounds of the patterns, which are thus shown to have been added to the glass surface and not the result of action by acid. The effect of this method of decoration is quite unlike the engraving it was meant to imitate, and it is entirely pleasing; but it remained a hand process, and the difficulty of fusing the coating to the glass, without melting it, must have limited its usefulness as a commercial innovation.

Another novelty of the early part of the century, and one which attracted a good deal of attention, was the making of 'cameo incrustations' or (to use a simpler term) objects containing 'sulphides'. In 1819 Apsley Pellatt (the younger) of the firm of Pellatt & Green in London patented several methods of embedding these small white-paste figures, usually busts, into objects made of clear glass. He originally described this work as Crystallo-Ceramie, and later as 'cameo incrustations'. Where it was appropriate the glassware containing these figures was finished with fine quality cutting (Plate 50). From the personalities represented in surviving examples it can be deduced that most of Apsley Pellatt's sulphides were made during the years immediately following the issue of the patent, although their making must have continued for some time afterwards and examples were included in the firm's display at the 1851 exhibition.[3] As Pellatt himself makes quite clear in his book *The Curiosities of Glass Making* (1849), his conception of the 'cameo incrustations' was by no means original, and was derived directly from continental antecedents. In this book he describes in detail his methods of manufacture, and it can be readily envisaged that the difficulties caused by the differing rates of contraction and the necessity of removing air bubbles from the face of the ceramic inserts must have resulted in a high proportion of wastage. The Apsley Pellatt sulphides were probably not a commercial success; but they were widely known, and the process was used elsewhere later in the century, particularly by the firm of John Ford at the Holyrood glassworks in Edinburgh (Plate 51).

It will be noticed that the glasses with coated decoration and those with sulphides were made of clear colourless material. Comparatively little is heard of the use of coloured or obscured glasses among the fashionable wares until about the time when the excise was removed in 1845; but on the other hand it is perhaps important to emphasize that such glasses were not by any means unknown during this period. Early price lists which have survived in the possession of the firm of Stevens & Williams at Brierley Hill, near Stourbridge, contain many instances of coloured glasses being used for layered, or cased, glassware, and as an alternative material for cut-glass patterns, in a context which appears to be about the middle thirties. Also in the mid-thirties the Dudley firm of Thomas Hawkes was making 'gold enamel' ware, such as the 'splendid gold enamel desert [*sic*] service, furnished to the corporation of London on her Majesty's first

[3] From about 1831 the firm became 'Pellatt & Co.' or 'Apsley Pellatt'.

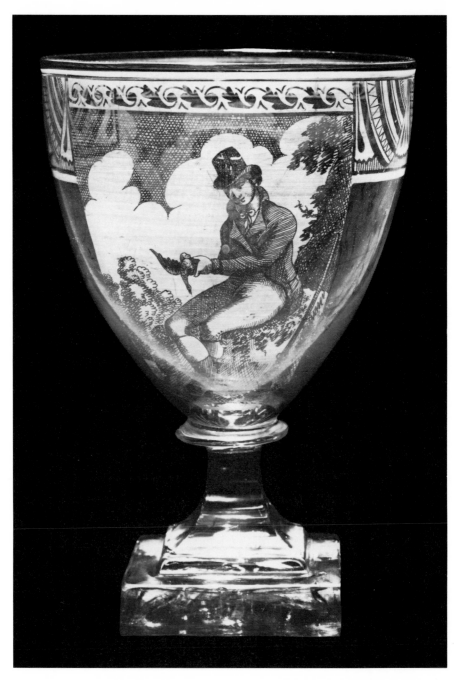

49. GOBLET with decoration drawn on a powdered-glass coating, marked on the base 'Patent'. Ht. 15.6 cm (6.1 in). Probably made by the Davenport firm at Longport, STOKE-ON-TRENT, about 1810. *National Museum of Antiquities of Scotland. See page 53*

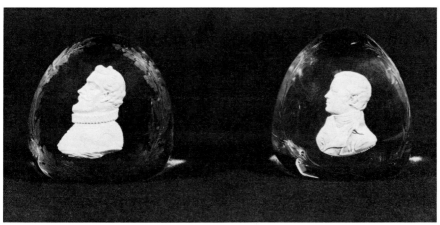

50. CUP, with sulphides representing the Prince Regent and King George III. Probably made by Pellatt & Green, LONDON, about 1820. *By gracious permission of H.M. The Queen. See pages 29, 57*

51. Two beehive-shaped PAPERWEIGHTS, decorated with engraving and containing sulphides of George Heriot and Robert Burns respectively. Hts. 5.7 cm (2.25 in) and 6 cm (2.4 in). Made by John Ford, EDINBURGH, perhaps about 1875. *Royal Scottish Museum. See page 57*

visit to the Guildhall, on the 9th November, 1837' (Colour Plate A).[4] About the early forties the current styles of cutting and engraving were being used in conjunction with surface stains, particularly it seems the ruby-red derived from copper rather than the yellowish-brown from silver (Plates 52(a), 83). This was the period which on the Continent saw a remarkable development in the technique and styles of using coloured and obscured glasses. In Central Europe the movement perhaps represented a reaction against the dominating influence of the British Regency style of cut glass in the first quarter of the century. It may be said to have begun in the twenties with the development in Bohemia of the heavily coloured opaque glasses known as 'hyalith' and 'lithyalin'. Such glasses were unsuited for decoration by mitre cutting and the plain vertical facet cutting used for their decoration was clearly connected with the broad-fluted style of cutting crystal glass. The glass made in Central Europe during the twenties, thirties and forties is known by the term 'Biedermeier', which is equally applied to the other arts of the period; and among the glassmaking techniques associated with it were those, which have been already mentioned, of firing coloured stains into the surface, or else of colouring glasses by forming them of contrasting layers. These coloured glass techniques and styles were taken up by glass factories in other Western European countries, and particularly by those in France, which during the later thirties and forties produced a great deal of attractive wares in the semi-opaque white and coloured 'opaline' glasses.

The reluctance of the British manufacturers to take any leading part in these international fashions was partly due no doubt to the restrictive effect of the methods whereby the excise was collected. We may suspect that it was also due in some degree to a certain conservative regard for the virtues of their fine lead crystal. By the forties, however, the potential interest in coloured and opaline glasses, and in their adjuncts of painting and gilding, was becoming irresistible. Quite suddenly the British manufacturers responded wholeheartedly to the demand for colour and began to make a belated contribution to the international Biedermeier styles. In this movement one personality stood out before all others, that of Benjamin Richardson, of the Stourbridge firm of W. H., B. & J. Richardson, who was later to be referred to as 'the father of the glass trade'.[5] In an exhibition held in Manchester at the end of the very year in which the excise had been removed, the Richardson display included clear coloured, opaline, layered and painted pieces.[6] In this the firm was foreshadowing most of the methods of using colour which were to occupy a great part of its efforts, and the efforts of other firms, during the few crowded years up to the Great Exhibition of 1851.

[4]*Bentley's History etc. of Dudley*, Birmingham, *c.* 1840, pp. 49–50. See also *Pottery Gazette*, 1888, p. 605.
[5]*Pottery Gazette*, 1888, p. 50.
[6]'Exposition of British Industrial Art' held in 1845/46 in connection with the Manchester School of Design, *Art Union*, 1846, p. 23 et seq.

52. Two WINEGLASSES, each cut
with flat flutes on a drop stem:
(a) ruby stained on the flutes
only, (b) of deep green glass.
Hts. 9.7 cm (3.8 in) and
13.4 cm (5.25 in). Probably
made in the 1840s by W. H., B.
& J. Richardson, STOURBRIDGE.
Stourbridge Glass Collection.
See pages 33, 60, 62

53. JUG of layered glass, opaque
white over crystal, with cut
decoration. Ht. 20.3 cm (8 in).
About 1845. *Stourbridge Glass
Collection. See page 62*

In an exhibition held in Birmingham in 1849 all the outstanding Birmingham firms were represented, as well as Richardson's of Stourbridge; and it is clear both from the catalogue and from contemporary accounts that coloured and opaline glass formed the most significant part of the displays of the leading firms of George Bacchus & Sons, Rice Harris & Son and Lloyd & Summerfield.[7] Only F. & C. Osler, who were concentrating on large-scale work in cut glass, were not showing any coloured glass, although in the previous year they had been noticed in the *Art Union* for their 'opal' flower vases with painted relief patterns shown in an exhibition at the Royal Polytechnic Institution in London.[8] The culmination of the fashion came with the 1851 exhibition, at which nearly all the glass manufacturers of standing were showing some coloured wares. The *Official Descriptive and Illustrated Catalogue* of the exhibition lists the colours to be found on the stands of three of them — Davis, Greathead & Green of Stourbridge, Rice Harris, and Bacchus.[9] The list of Rice Harris is slightly the longest and is given as 'opal, alabaster, turquoise, amber, canary, topaz, chrysoprase, pink, blue, light and dark ruby, black, brown, green, purple etc.'. Most newspaper and magazine critics of the work of the British glassmakers at the various exhibitions around 1850 were inclined to find their coloured glass promising but not yet quite the equal of Bohemian glass. This would not in any case be surprising, in view of the short period during which the British manufacturers had been seriously concerned with coloured glass. Some of the colour was used in a manner which was unmistakably British; but often the style of the coloured and opaline work was scarcely distinguishable from that of Bohemia or France.

Clear coloured glass might be used for any of the styles of glasswork for which clear crystal glass was used (Plate 52(b)); and it was the characteristic material for small objects, such as toilet bottles, which were cut with broad vertical facets on angular shapes in the manner of contemporary Bohemian work. The most striking use of colour was, however, in layered glass. The body of a vessel might be in clear uncoloured glass covered by a single layer of opaque-white or coloured glass (Plates 53, 54); or it might consist of several layers of glasses of contrasting colours, while a layer of opaque-white glass might be used to emphasize the change of colour between two transparent glasses (Plate 55). It was natural for layered glass to be given cut decoration. Sometimes this took the form of mitre cutting (Colour Plate B); but usually it consisted of spaced hollows or broad vertical facets, and these might be given a pointed or cusped outline such as to suggest the shape of individual lights in Gothic traceried windows (Plate 55).

---

[7] 'Exhibition of Manufactures and Art' held on the occasion of a meeting of the British Association for the Advancement of Science, *Art Journal*, 1849, p. 293 et seq.; *Journal of Design and Manufactures*, vol. II (1849–50), passim.
[8] *Art Union*, 1848, p. 162.
[9] Vol. II, pp. 699–700.

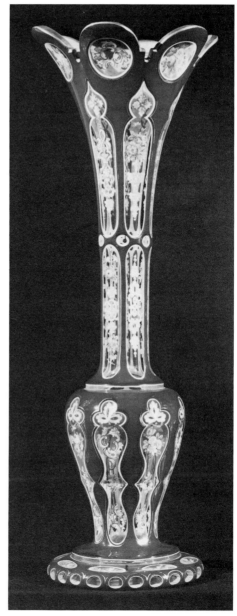

54. TOILET BOTTLE of layered glass, blue over crystal, with cut decoration. Ht. 18.3 cm (7.25 in). Made by Apsley Pellatt, LONDON, 1851. *Photograph by the Musée des Techniques, Conservatoire National des Arts et Métiers, Paris. See page 62*

55. VASE of layered glass, blue and opaque white over crystal, with cut panels painted and gilded. Ht. 40.6 cm (16 in). Apparently made by W. H., B. & J. Richardson, STOURBRIDGE, about 1848. *Stourbridge Glass Collection (Victoria and Albert Museum photograph). See page 62*

In many instances the layered glass was further embellished by painting, gilding or engraving, either on the undisturbed portions of the outer surface or on the surfaces exposed in the shallow cuts. Layering could also be used in the same way as staining to provide a coloured ground for engraving which would cut through it into crystal glass below; and a layered surface would be preferred to a stained one for the more ambitious deeply-cut engraving such as that produced by W. J. Muckley for the Richardson display at the 1851 exhibition (Plate 85).[10]

In contrast with much of the plain-coloured and layered work, the opalines were usually made in the soft curving shapes which were more appropriate than angular shapes to the mid-century spirit of design. Since opaline glass was not transparent and had little light-reflecting quality, there was little point in cutting it, and glassmakers tended to use it in a manner which was natural to furnace manipulation, including on occasion the trailed-on decoration of coiling snakes. Versions of French opaline styles seem to have been made by several Midland firms, although it may not be easy to distinguish British from continental work. These included porcelain-like vases painted and gilded with loose overall flower designs. Some of these made by Richardson's about 1851 have been claimed as the work of Thomas Bott, who later distinguished himself by painting in a very different style on Worcester porcelain (Plate 56);[11] but a surviving Richardson pattern shows that at least some work in this manner was carried out by a painter named Lawrence, who is apparently to be equated with Stephen Lawrence, a former Coalport porcelain painter.[12]

Most of the British painted work, however, was carried out in a less ambitious manner on simple jugs and vases in a taste which was distinctive of this country. The jugs are especially characteristic of the place and the period. Their shapes are reminiscent of contemporary pottery, and the frequently recurring three-lipped mouth is derived from the British revival of interest in Greek pottery during the forties. For most of this work white opaline glass was used, either the sort which was known specifically as white opal or else the slightly greyish variety known as alabaster glass. The surface of the vessels was often roughened by abrasion; and this presumably had the advantage of improving the surface as a ground for decoration. Surviving examples from the Richardson factory (they are often identified by a printed inscription on the base) include glasses with tightly painted flowers in a style used on contemporary porcelain, with plain gilded motifs and with scenes painted in sepia monochrome or in colours (Plates 57–9). One of the painted white opalines illustrated here is from the Lambeth firm of J. F. Christy,

[10]For W. J. Muckley see p. 86.
[11]*Detailed Catalogue of . . . a Loan Exhibition of Stourbridge Glass*, Stourbridge (1951), Nos. 71 and 73, the latter being the subject of Plate 56.
[12]G. A. Godden, *Coalport and Coalbrookdale Porcelains*, London (1970), p. 97. The Richardson pattern is in the possession of Dudley Metropolitan Borough.

A. 'Gold enamel' glass PLATE, decorated behind with cutting, printing, painting, gilding and possibly some acid etching. Diam. 22.5 cm (8.8 in). Probably made by the firm of Thomas Hawkes, DUDLEY, about 1837, and used for the reception of Queen Victoria by the Corporation of London. *Victoria and Albert Museum. See page 60*

B. DECANTER of layered glass, opaque white over ruby, with mitre cutting. Ht. 30.5 cm (12 in). Made by George Bacchus & Sons, BIRMINGHAM, about 1850. *Victoria and Albert Museum. See pages 33, 62*

56. White opaline VASE with painted decoration and gilding. Ht. 44.1 cm
(17.4 in). Made by W. H., B. & J. Richardson, STOURBRIDGE (marked),
about 1850. *Stourbridge Glass Collection (Victoria and Albert Museum photograph).*
See page 64

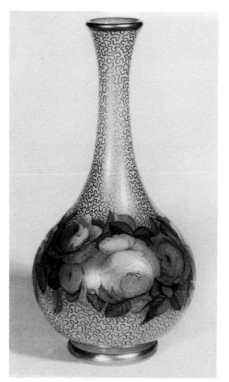

57. White opaline VASE with painted rose decoration on a gilded vermiculated ground. Ht. 26.7 cm (10.5 in). Apparently made by the firm of Benjamin Richardson, STOURBRIDGE, about 1855. *Stourbridge Glass Collection.* *See page 64*

58. White opaline JUG with gilded decoration. Ht. 23.9 cm (9.4 in). Made by W. H., B. & J. Richardson, STOURBRIDGE (marked), probably about 1850. *Stourbridge Glass Collection.* *See page 64*

59. White opaline JUG with roughened surface and monochrome sepia painting. Ht. 22.9 cm (9 in). Made by W. H., B. & J. Richardson, STOURBRIDGE (marked), about 1850. *Victoria and Albert Museum. See page 64*

60. White opaline VASE, painted and gilded. Ht. 32.7 cm (12.9 in). Made by J. F. Christy, LAMBETH (marked), about 1849. *Victoria and Albert Museum. See page 68*

which in 1849 was given an award by the Society of Arts for 'Specimens of Enamelled Glass' (Plate 60). For some of the humbler opalines, transfer printing was used, either by itself or with added colouring, and examples are illustrated here from the firms of Bacchus and Richardson (Plates 61–4).

Painting on clear colourless glass gave a very different effect from painting on opaline; and the use of clear glass had the theoretical advantage that a vessel's contents could still be seen between the painted motifs. Richardson's made considerable use of painting on jugs and drinking glasses which are attractively decorated with large scale representations of flowers or seaweed (Plates 65–7). George Hancock, the ceramic painter who had long been associated with the Derby factory, was working at Richardson's in the 1840s and this style of painting may well be attributed to him.[13] It is interesting to notice that most of the glassware designs among those commissioned by Henry Cole around 1847 for his 'Summerly's Art Manufactures' were for objects of clear glass with painted or gilded decoration. Some of these were made by Richardson's; but the best known, and certainly the most imitated, were the 'Well Spring' glasses which were designed by the easel painter Richard Redgrave and made by the firm of J. F. Christy. This design using a motif of water plants was an example of the current concept of 'suggestive ornament' since the objects in question were all intended for use with water (Colour Plate C).

This was an age when the decorative arts were prone to appear as museum-inspired imitations of past styles, and it is worth noticing therefore that glassware was comparatively little affected by this tendency. It may be suspected, however, that this fortunate circumstance was due mainly to the glassmakers' ignorance of historic glass styles which could be suitably copied. Probably the strongest historical influence upon the glassware of the mid-century came from a different medium, the pottery of Ancient Greece. Elements of Greek form and decoration were frequently recurring, and sometimes painted glass was produced to imitate both the decoration and the forms of Greek pottery. An example is illustrated here from the firm of J. F. Christy (Plate 68). At the 1851 exhibition painted glass versions of Greek pottery were shown by Davis, Greathead & Green of Stourbridge, and these were thought sufficiently noteworthy to figure among the very few illustrations of glassware in the *Official Descriptive and Illustrated Catalogue*. The historical Venetian glass of the sixteenth and seventeenth centuries was beginning to exert an influence during the later forties, in the sense that it was regarded as historically respectable and worthy of imitation. As yet the glassmakers' conception of Venetian glass was vague, although it probably improved a little after the showing of Venetian glass in the Society of Arts exhibition of Mediaeval Art in 1850. In his *Curiosities of Glass Making*, published in 1849, Apsley Pellatt described several of the Venetian techniques, and at the

[13] J. Haslem, *The Old Derby China Factory*, London (1876), p. 130.

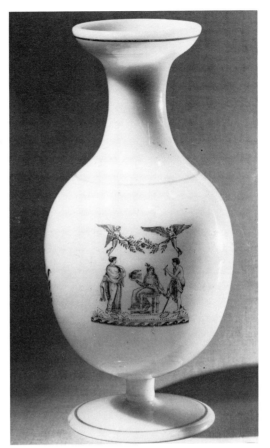

61. White opaline VASE with
transfer-printed decoration.
Ht. 25.4 cm (10 in). Made by
George Bacchus & Sons,
BIRMINGHAM (marked),
about 1850. *Location unknown.*
See page 68

62. White opaline TUMBLER, with
transfer-printed decoration, painted
and gilded. Ht. 11.1 cm (4.4 in).
Made by W. H., B. & J.
Richardson, STOURBRIDGE
(marked), about 1850. *Stourbridge
Glass Collection. See page 68*

63. White opaline VASE, with classical figures transfer-printed and gilded on a blue ground. Ht. 30.5 cm (12 in). Made by W. H., B. & J. Richardson, STOURBRIDGE (marked), and dated (by registry mark) 1847. *Stourbridge Glass Collection. See page 68*

64. Yellow opaline BOTTLE, transfer-printed with vine decoration and figures representing the word 'Gin'. Ht. 31.1 cm (12.25 in). Made by W. H., B. & J. Richardson, STOURBRIDGE (marked), about 1850. *Stourbridge Glass Collection. See page 68*

65. JUG and GOBLET, with painted decoration of seaweed. Ht. of jug 24.1 cm
(9.5 in). Made by W. H., B. & J. Richardson, STOURBRIDGE, about
1845–50. *Stourbridge Glass Collection. See page 68*

66. JUG and GOBLET, with painted decoration of irises. Ht. of jug 24.1 cm
(9.5 in). Made by W. H., B. & J. Richardson, STOURBRIDGE, about 1850.
Stourbridge Glass Collection. See page 68

67. JUG of clear colourless glass with painted decoration. Ht. 23.5 cm (9.25 in).
Made by W. H., B. & J. Richardson, STOURBRIDGE (marked). The piece
bears a registry mark of 1848. *Victoria and Albert Museum. See page 68*

68. VASE of black glass painted in red and black in imitation of Ancient Greek pottery. Ht. 32.7 cm (12.9 in). Made by J. F. Christy, LAMBETH, about 1849. *Victoria and Albert Museum. See page 68*

1851 exhibition his firm was showing ice-glass, or 'frosted' glass, described as 'Anglo-Venetian'. An example of Apsley Pellatt ice-glass, acquired in 1851, is illustrated here together with an example by Bacchus (Plates 69, 70). The practice of decorating glasses by embedding in them filigree glass canes—a practice associated with Venetian glass and with the glass of eighteenth-century England—was revived during the years immediately preceding the 1851 exhibition. Coloured or white filigree canes were used particularly in the stems of wineglasses, and the stems themselves were sometimes convoluted in a manner which was also derived from Venice. Examples are shown here from Bacchus and from Apsley Pellatt (Plates 86(b), 87(b)). A 'threaded Venetian stem' was noticed among the Richardson contributions to the Society of Arts exhibition in 1849. The firm of Rice Harris was also mentioned in 1849 for its 'threaded' glass,[14] and at the 1851 exhibition Bacchus and Osler.[15] At the 1851 exhibition elaborately convoluted stems were a feature of the display of Lloyd & Summerfield.[16]

Besides the many styles of glassware which were put into production for normal table and ornamental purposes, the years around the middle of the century saw a number of commercial novelties. Glass busts were being made by the two Birmingham firms of Osler and Lloyd & Summerfield. These were formed in moulds, and, at least in the case of the Osler examples, were given a roughened surface by abrading. Both firms made versions of Queen Victoria and of Prince Albert (Plate 71). The Osler list included also Shakespeare, Milton, Scott, Peel and a statuette called A Sleeping Child. Lloyd & Summerfield extended the idea to include glass busts in medallion form. Another novelty was provided by the silvered glasses made with double walls, which were silvered on the inside surfaces. These were often layered with a coloured glass on the outside, so that cutting or engraving would expose the clear silvered glass below; but the attractions of this double-walled glassware were limited to its surface appearance, and rarely did the designers or makers succeed in achieving any elegance of shape. The British patent which covered the production of this glass was taken out in December 1849 by F. Hale Thomson and Edward Varnish;[17] the manufacturers were apparently James Powell & Sons of the Whitefriars glassworks in London (Colour Plate D).[18]

The best remembered novelty, however, of the mid-century period is that of the millefiori paperweights, although to contemporaries they rarely seemed worthy of serious comment and they were to be bought in stationers' shops rather

---

[14] Art Journal, 1849, p. 65. For the usual sense of 'threading', see page 113.
[15] Official Descriptive and Illustrated Catalogue, vol. II, p. 699 and 700.
[16] The Art Journal Illustrated Catalogue . . . 1851, p. 270.
[17] Patent No. 12905, 19 December 1849.
[18] Art Journal, 1851, p. 76; Tallis's History and Description of the Crystal Palace, London and New York (1851), vol. I, p. 82.

69. FINGER BOWL of ice-glass.
Ht. 10 cm (4 in). Made by
Apsley Pellatt, LONDON,
1851. *Photograph by the Musée
des Techniques, Conservatoire
National des Arts et Métiers,
Paris. See page 74*

70. VASE of ice-glass, with
embedded fragments of
coloured and opaque white
glasses and with gilded bands.
Ht. 18.4 cm (7.25 in). Made
by George Bacchus & Sons,
BIRMINGHAM, about 1853.
*Victoria and Albert Museum.
See page 74*

71. BUST OF PRINCE ALBERT, moulded and slightly cut, with roughened surface, inscribed 'Published by F. & C. Osler, 44 Oxford St., London May 1st 1845'. Ht. 24.5 cm (9.6 in). Made by F. & C. Osler, BIRMINGHAM. *Victoria and Albert Museum. See page 74*

than from glass and china dealers.[19] The fashion for them came from France, where they had been made since 1845 and whence they were imported into Britain in great numbers. The French makers developed many techniques for filling the weights with interesting and colourful motifs; but most of the weights of this period which can be reasonably presumed to be British are of the sort which uses millefiori decoration, that is, the base of the weight contains embedded in the colourless glass an arrangement of small coloured glass canes. The curiosity of these weights lay in the magnification of the pattern by the overlying glass; and, once acquired, the technique of millefiori patterning could be used with similar effect in any glass objects, such as standing inkwells or glass doorknobs, which offered the same opportunities for magnification through thick glass. Reference was made to the manufacture of paperweights by Bacchus in the *Art Union* at the end of 1848[20] and in the *Journal of Design and Manufactures* during 1849.[21] In 1849 this firm was also showing paperweights (described as 'letter weights') at the Birmingham exhibition, and from the carefully compiled catalogue it seems that they were the only firm to do so. But a reference in the *Art Journal* at the beginning of 1849 shows that another Birmingham firm, Rice Harris, was also making them at that time,[22] and the Stourbridge firm of Richardson was showing a 'cut glass paper weight' among the material sent to the 1849 exhibition of the Society of Arts.[23] The Rice Harris factory was known as the Islington Glass Works, and some weights with canes lettered 'IGW' are presumably the product of this factory (Colour Plate E). The use of coloured filigree glass canes, particularly for wineglass stems (see above, page 74), may have been connected with the use of similar canes for millefiori paperweights, and it may be suspected that the firms which produced filigree stems may have experimented with paperweights, even though they may not have put them into production.

Some rough green paperweights or doorstops, known as 'dumps', from the north of England should be mentioned here, since they expressed at the most popular level the idea of enclosing a pattern within a solid mass of glass. These were of tall beehive shape, made of green bottle glass and enclosing most often the airy pattern of a flower (Plate 72) or else an arrangement of spaced bubbles. A few of these bear the stamp 'J. Kilner/Maker/Wakefield' (or in a rare instance 'J. Kilner & Sons/Makers/Wakefield'). It can be assumed that these marked pieces were made before the firm became known as Kilner Brothers on John Kilner's

[19] *Journal of Design and Manufactures*, vol. I (1849), p. 95.
[20] p. 343.
[21] Vol. I, p. 95.
[22] p. 65. The *Art Union* was renamed the *Art Journal* at the beginning of 1849.
[23] *A Catalogue of Specimens of Recent British Manufactures and Decorative Art . . .*, Society of Arts, London (1849).

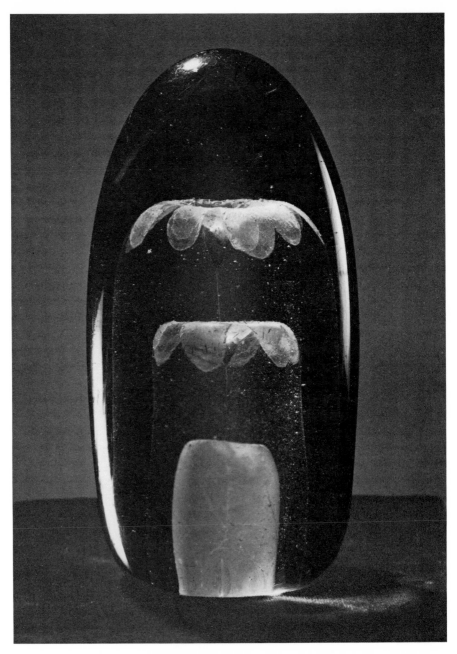

72. PAPERWEIGHT or 'DUMP' of green bottle glass enclosing a flower pattern. Ht. 12.7 cm (5 in). Probably made in the NORTH OF ENGLAND, in the middle or later nineteenth century. *Victoria and Albert Museum. See page 77*

death in 1857,[24] while other unmarked examples may have been made in his glassworks at a later date. Some examples enclosed ceramic figures in the manner of sulphides; one enclosing a ceramic bust, apparently of Queen Victoria, is stated to have been made at the 1887 Jubilee in a glassworks at Knottingley, which is also in West Yorkshire.[25]

[24] *The British Trade Journal*, 1 December 1894.
[25] In the Tolson Memorial Museum, Huddersfield.

3

Engraved Glass

Of the methods whereby glassware could be decorated, engraving was probably the one which answered best to Victorian taste. It was the most appropriate means of expressing on glass a feeling for close complicated patterns and for naturalistic and pictorial effects. Very little distinguished engraved work had been carried out in Britain in earlier times; but from the middle of the nineteenth century British glass-manufacturers and dealers began to produce a great amount of fine engraved work using many distinct techniques, and the significance of this development was in no way diminished by the help which they got from Central European craftsmen.

In the early decades of the century simple wheel-engraved motifs appeared often enough on wineglasses and were accompanied on larger vessels by the lettering of mottoes and inscriptions. Floral and other plant motifs were sometimes used effectively and with some elaboration (Plates 74, 75, 77); but figure subjects were unusual and appeared only on special pieces (Plate 73). This was the heyday of cut glass, and it is clear from the manner in which engraving was used, and from the avoidance of difficult subject matter, that it was considered useful only for ornamenting the bowls of wineglasses, where cutting could not reasonably be used, and for the special purpose of producing commemorative pieces. Much of the early-century engraving was carried out on the current rummer and goblet shape with convex sides (Plates 73, 74), or on shapes which in origin reach back further into the eighteenth century (Plate 75); but the straight-sided bucket shape soon became the favourite for engraved work and especially for commemorative and souvenir glasses (Plates 76–81). This was the shape mainly used for the Sunderland glasses depicting the famous bridge (Plate 76), which were made in great numbers during the twenties, thirties and forties, although the bridge had been opened as long ago as 1796. Similar glass was engraved in Newcastle upon Tyne (Plate 79); a goblet illustrated here has naively rendered figures engraved by Thomas Hudson, who worked in that town from the mid-thirties to the early fifties (Plate 80). By 1840 a bell-shaped goblet might be used for a commemoration (Plate 84), although the bucket shape was still being used for engraving, especially in the

C. The 'Well Spring' WATER CARAFE, painted and gilt. Ht. 26 cm (10.25 in).
Made for Henry Cole's 'Summerly's Art Manufactures' by J. F. Christy,
LAMBETH (marked). The decoration was designed by Richard Redgrave; it
was registered in 1847 and the piece bears the registry mark. *Victoria and Albert
Museum. See pages 68, 94*

D. Silvered glass GOBLET and STANDING BOWL, green and ruby layered respectively, with cut decoration. Hts. 22.5 cm (8.8 in) and 18.4 cm (7.25 in). Made for E. Varnish, LONDON (marked), about 1850. *Victoria and Albert Museum. See page 74*

E. Millefiori PAPERWEIGHT. Diam. 7 cm (2.75 in). One of the canes bears the letters 'IGW' which is presumed to indicate manufacture at the Islington glassworks (Rice Harris & Son), BIRMINGHAM, about 1850. *The John Nelson Bergstrom Art Center and Mahler Glass Museum, Neenah, Wisconsin. See page 77*

73. Engraved WINEGLASS
commemorating the battle of
Trafalgar (1805). Ht. 14 cm
(5.5 in). *Victoria and Albert
Museum. See pages 22, 80*

74. Engraved GOBLET, dated
1805. Ht. 19.7 cm (7.75 in).
*Victoria and Albert Museum.
See pages 22, 80*

75. Engraved LOVING-CUP. A
coin of 1817 is enclosed in the
knop of its stem. Ht. 20 cm
(7.9 in). *Tyne and Wear County
Council Museums (Laing Art
Gallery, Newcastle upon Tyne).
See page 80*

76. GOBLET with cut decoration
and engraved with Sunderland
Bridge and Sunderland
Exchange (opened in 1796 and
1814 respectively). Ht. 26.3 cm
(10.4 in). Probably made about
1825. *Tyne and Wear County
Council Museums (Sunderland
Museum). See page 80*

82

77. Engraved GOBLET with legend 'No grumbling'. Ht. 19.7 cm (7.75 in). Probably made about 1830. *Victoria and Albert Museum. See page 80*

78. WINEGLASS with engraving of a named yacht. Ht. 11.7 cm (4.6 in). From its subject the engraving can be dated about 1839–40. *Victoria and Albert Museum. See page 80*

79. GOBLET engraved with the Tyne
suspension bridge (opened in 1831).
Ht. 26.7 cm (10.5 in). Probably made about
1835. *Tyne and Wear County Council
Museums (Laing Art Gallery, Newcastle upon
Tyne). See page 80*

80. GOBLET engraved with Neptune and
seahorses, signed by T. (Thomas) Hudson,
Newcastle. Ht. 22.9 cm (9 in). Probably
made about 1840. *Tyne and Wear County
Council Museums (Laing Art Gallery,
Newcastle upon Tyne). See page 80*

81. WINEGLASS with diamond-point
engraving presumably carried out in
SCOTLAND. The engraving includes a
shield bearing carpenter's tools, a personal
inscription and the date 1830. Ht. 10.8 cm
(4.25 in). *Royal Scottish Museum. See pages 80,*

82. BOTTLE of deep-green glass chip-engraved with a scene including the motto
'Speed the Plough'; on the obverse are the arms of the Earl of Stirling and
round the base the inscription 'Engraved by D. Erskine, Alloa, 1840'.
Ht. 30.5 cm (12 in). *Smith Art Gallery and Museum, Stirling (photograph Tom Scott).*
See page 86

north-east of England. Diamond-point engraving was practised, although less commonly, and is illustrated here by a Scottish example of 1830 (Plate 81). From Scotland came also chip engravings, made with a sharp hammer on bottle glass, which were associated especially with the glasshouse in Alloa (Plate 82).

With the thirties and forties the scope of engraved work seems to have widened. Members of the Herbert family of Dudley, and particularly William Herbert, were attracting attention during the thirties for the engravings which they were carrying out for the Dudley firm of Thomas Hawkes (see page 102). In the nearby Stourbridge district the Wood family had an important engraving shop about the forties, and Thomas Wood produced an independent display for the 1851 exhibition. Two surviving examples of the work of a member of this family are a floral design and a tropical festival scene engraved on ruby-stained bottles (Plate 83).

Wheel-engraving was well suited for decorating the Victorian globular decanters and water carafes (Plate 89); and the development of these shapes about the early years of Victoria's reign no doubt tended to encourage the use of engraving. Another new shape, the hemispherical or saucer champagne glass, was even more closely associated with engraving since it could scarcely be decorated by any form of cutting (Plate 86). On the popular shapes of the later forties, such as the jugs with rounded bodies and the water carafes, one often finds versions of the loose-running plant patterns which appear in relief on contemporary pottery (Plate 89). One of the most charming examples of mid-century work is a sensitively composed flower-engraving on a ruby-layered goblet from the Richardson factory, which may have been shown at the 1851 exhibition and is now in the Stourbridge Glass Collection (Plate 85 and see page 64). This piece is attributed to W. J. Muckley, who is described in the *Art Journal* catalogue of the exhibition as the firm's 'principal designer and engraver'.[1]

The most significant engraved glass at the 1851 exhibition, however, was the work shown by the London dealers, and in particular by the firm of J. G. (Joseph George) Green. One fine piece from this firm's display was the 'Neptune' jug, a large Greek 'oenochoe' shape with high shoulder, spreading foot and three-lipped mouth, and with the greater part of its surface covered by elaborately engraved figure compositions (Plate 88). This piece was much illustrated at the time in accounts of the exhibition, and it is fortunate that it has survived in the Victoria and Albert Museum.

The Greek 'oenochoe' shape was to have a very wide currency later in the century, but the most usual shapes for engraved decanters, claret jugs and vases

---

[1] *Art Journal Illustrated Catalogue . . . 1851*, p. 138. See also *Detailed Catalogue of . . . a Loan Exhibition of Stourbridge Glass*, Stourbridge (1951), no. 54. W. J. Muckley was presumably related to, but not identical with, the later nineteenth-century easel painter William Jabez Muckley, who was apparently born in 1837.

83. Two ruby-stained BOTTLES. Hts. 30.5 cm (12 in) and 29.8 cm (11.75 in). Engraved by a member of the Wood family of Brettell Lane, near Stourbridge, about 1840–50. *Mrs M. E. Southall (a relation of the Wood family). See pages 60, 86*

84. Engraved GOBLET, dated 1840. Ht. 16.5 cm (6.5 in). *Victoria and Albert Museum. See pages 33, 80*

85. GOBLET with engraved ruby-layered bowl. Ht. 19.7 cm (7.75 in). Made by W. H., B. & J. Richardson, STOURBRIDGE, and said to have been shown at the 1851 exhibition. Designed and perhaps engraved by W. J. Muckley. *Stourbridge Glass Collection (Victoria and Albert Museum photograph). See pages 33, 64, 86*

86. CHAMPAGNE GLASSES with engraved bowls: (a) with plain stem, (b) with double looped filigree stem. Hts. 11.7 cm (4.6 in) and 12.7 cm (5 in). Made by George Bacchus & Sons, BIRMINGHAM, about 1850. *Victoria and Albert Museum. See pages 74, 86*

87. Two WINEGLASSES: (a) with engraved decoration, (b) with filigree stem. Hts. 14 cm (5.5 in) and 15 cm (5.9 in). Made by (a) F. & C. Osler, BIRMINGHAM, (b) Apsley Pellatt, LONDON. Acquired in 1851. *Photograph by the Musée des Techniques, Conservatoire National des Arts et Métiers, Paris. See pages 33, 74*

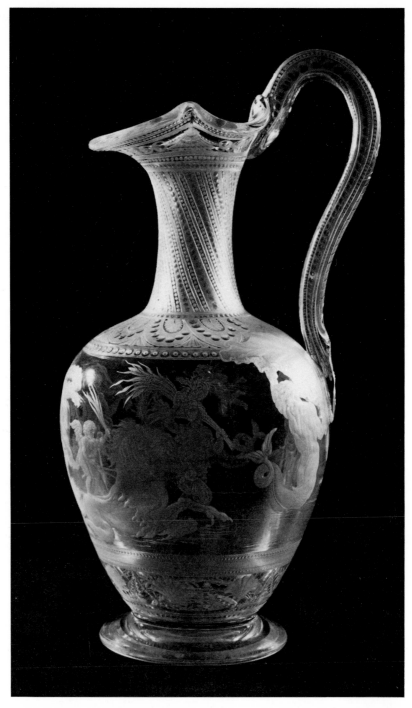

88. 'Neptune' JUG. Ht. 33.7 cm (13.25 in). Shown at the 1851 exhibition by the London dealer J. G. Green. *Victoria and Albert Museum. See pages 86, 94*

89. Engraved WATER CARAFE with matching TUMBLER. Ht. 15.3 cm (6 in). Made by F. & C. Osler, BIRMINGHAM, 1851. *Photograph by the Musée des Techniques, Conservatoire National des Arts et Métiers, Paris. See page 86*

90. Engraved JUG (oval in section). Ht. 26.7 cm (10.5 in). Bought about 1869 from the London dealers W. P. & G. Phillips and Pearce. *Victoria and Albert Museum. See page 92*

during the later fifties, sixties and early seventies were footed ovoid shapes which looked best when blown thinly and which offered a large area for engraving (Plates 90, 91). Another shape much used for engraving in the sixties was the tankard-shaped water jug with straight slightly tapering sides. This shape was often used as a field for fine engraving until near the end of the century (Plates 92, 93), but has since become too banal for such treatment. The greater part of the engraving of the sixties consisted of Renaissance arabesques or else of motifs derived from Greek sources, while naturalistically treated designs with flowers, birds and hunting scenes became increasingly common in the later sixties and seventies. Figure-engraving was most often classically inspired, and it was naturally less common than formal or floral motifs. This was the period when wheel engraving was by far the most significant type of decoration on fashionable glassware; it was also the period when the London producers and dealers exerted their greatest influence, and their displays of engraved glass dominated the British glassware especially at the London exhibition of 1862. Besides the glassmaking firm of Apsley Pellatt with its showrooms in Baker Street (usually known in the sixties simply as Pellatt & Co.), the London firms included, in 1862, W. P. & G. Phillips (of Oxford Street and New Bond Street), Dobson & Pearce (the successors of Joseph G. Green in St. James's Street), Naylor & Co. (of Princes Street, Cavendish Square) and James Green (of Upper Thames Street).[2] The list of dealers in glassware included also the china manufacturers W. T. Copeland who, with a London showroom in New Bond Street, were likewise commissioning and displaying engraved glassware at the international exhibitions.

The demand for engraved glass naturally attracted craftsmen from Central Europe, where there had been a strong tradition in this craft since the seventeenth century. They must have been responsible for much of the engraved work carried out in London. One well-publicized instance was a vase shown by Copeland's at the Universal Exhibition of Vienna in 1873. This was engraved by Paul Oppitz, the design being 'arranged' by J. Jones, one of the Copeland artists (Plate 91).[3] About the end of the fifties an emigrant Bohemian, J. H. B. Millar, set up in Edinburgh a workshop which he staffed initially with fellow Bohemian engravers. This workshop, which seems rapidly to have grown into a considerable concern, was closely connected with the firm of John Ford of the Holyrood glassworks; and at the exhibitions of London in 1862 and Paris in 1867 the work was displayed by John Millar, an apparently separate firm of Edinburgh dealers. The illustrations in the *Art Journal* catalogues show ambitious figure subjects, and (in the case of the 1862 exhibition) the fern

[2] J. B. Waring, *Masterpieces ... at the International Exhibition, 1862*, London (1863), vol. II, plate 142, confuses the two Green firms, which in the London directories appear distinct.
[3] *Art Journal*, 1873, pp. 156 and 295.

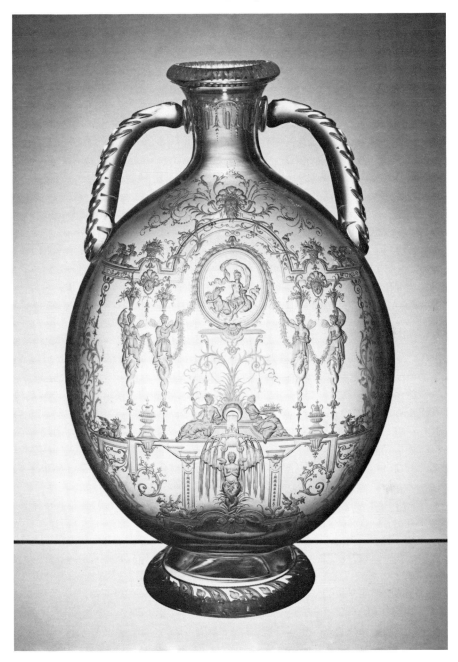

91. Engraved VASE. Ht. 28.3 cm (11.1 in). The decoration was 'arranged' by J. Jones and engraved by Paul Oppitz (inscribed on base). Shown by W. T Copeland & Sons at the Vienna exhibition of 1873. *Victoria and Albert Museum.* *See page 92*

patterns, which were a notable feature of the dealer's display and which were popular over a long period (Plate 92).[4] Emanuel Lerche was another of the Central European immigrants to Scotland, and his work also is illustrated here by a fern-pattern jug (Plate 93). Similarly in Dublin distinguished engraving was being carried out by Franz Tieze for the Pugh Glass Works and in Glasgow by H. Keller for the firm of John Baird (Plate 94).

In Stourbridge the most distinguished engraver during the sixties, and one of the most prominent during the remainder of the century, was the Bohemian Frederick E. Kny. He was connected with Thomas Webb & Sons, on whose premises he had a separate workshop. Like other engravers of the latter part of the century, he often engraved the well-known three-lipped decanter shape (Plate 95). This footed shape, with its high shoulder, its mouth pinched into three lips and its spherical stopper (usually with a tiny ball finial), was an outcome of the current regard for the purity of Greek pottery shapes, and its success was probably due to its suitability for engraving. Although other methods of decoration were used, it was a shape which looked well only when blown thin, and which seemed to call for the cool dignity of wheel-engraving. The Greek elements in the shape had been used before, as in Henry Cole's water carafe and J. G. Green's 1851 'Neptune' jug (Colour Plate C, Plate 88); and, except for an incongruous stopper, it appears complete as a handleless decanter among many others in the illustrations of Apsley Pellatt's display at the 1862 exhibition. But it was in the early seventies that this decanter shape, complete with the spherical stopper, suddenly burst into general popularity. In the Stourbridge district it appears in the pattern books of the firm of Stevens & Williams in January 1871 and in those of the Thomas Webb and Richardson firms (which are less exactly dated) about the same time. Thereafter it was constantly repeated in the pattern books with various decorations, and by the last decade of the century it had become internationally one of the most significant shapes in glass tableware.[5]

About the beginning of the eighties a new style of engraving appeared, known as 'rock crystal', which in the period of the Brilliant cut glass (see page 45) provided an even more sumptuous method of decorating clear lead table glass and ornamental objects. The most obvious characteristic of 'rock crystal' engraving is that the engraved lines and areas are polished in such a way that the whole surface of the vessel is uniformly bright, as compared with normal wheel-engraving, which is left unpolished to contrast with the surrounding surface. This technical change implied a distinctive approach to the design of engraved decoration. Instead of being a pattern on the surface of the glass the engraving tended to embrace almost the whole surface of the vessel, to become deeper and to assume virtually the character of carving. In this respect 'rock crystal' engraving

[4] David Bremner, *The Industries of Scotland*, Edinburgh (1869), p. 385.
[5] Elisa Steenberg, *Svenskt Adertonhundratals Glas*, Stockholm (1952), pp. 87 and 256.

92. JUG engraved with fern patterns. Ht. 24.8 cm (9.75 in). From the firm of John Ford, EDINBURGH, about the 1880s. *Huntly House Museum, Edinburgh. See pages 92, 94*

93. JUG engraved with fern patterns. Ht. 22.5 cm (8.8 in). Engraved by Emanuel Lerche and dated 1888 (the blank may have been imported). *National Museum of Antiquities of Scotland. See pages 92, 94*

94. JUG. Ht. 31.4 cm (12.4 in). Engraved by H. Keller at the firm of John Baird, GLASGOW, about 1886. *Art Gallery and Museum, Glasgow. See pages 94, 98*

95. DECANTER with shallow engraving. Ht. 30.8 cm (12.1 in). Engraved by Frederick E. Kny working at Thomas Webb & Sons, STOURBRIDGE. Probably made in the later 1870s. *Victoria and Albert Museum. See page 94*

was in keeping with the simultaneous development of carved cameo glass, which will be described later.

The firm of Thomas Webb held a strong reputation for 'rock crystal' work, and this formed part of the great extension of the firm's activities in the seventies and eighties under the energetic direction of Thomas Wilkes Webb and under the art-directorship of James O'Fallon, who was himself an engraver of distinction. At the Paris exhibition of 1878 the firm won the only Grand Prix for glass, and it is clear that it was from contact with France about the time of this exhibition that the firm derived its concept of 'rock crystal'.[6] A writer in the *Art Journal* catalogue of the exhibition discusses the fashion for deep engraving on thick glass and the work shown by such French firms as the Cristallerie de Pantin and the dealers 'A l'Escalier de Cristal' who 'have produced bold floral patterns, with birds and other objects, in this deep engraving, which is brilliantly polished'. The words 'rock crystal' were used in Thomas Webb's pattern books as early as July 1878 of pieces produced by Frederick Kny. In 1879 the name William Fritsche, another immigrant engraver, was also associated with this work and he may have been the innovator at Thomas Webb's.[7] Like Kny, Fritsche set up his own workshop at the Thomas Webb factory, and the production of 'rock crystal' engravings continued to be a major concern of these two workshops throughout the eighties and nineties (Plates 96, 97). A particularly distinguished example is the great fanciful jug made by Fritsche which is now in the Corning Museum of Glass, New York (Plate 98).

At Stevens & Williams the words 'rock crystal' were being used in the pattern books from 1879,[8] and examples were shown at the Wolverhampton exhibition of 1884.[9] A Central European engraver, Joseph Keller, was concerned with some of the 'rock crystal' work at Stevens & Williams, as was also an English engraver John Orchard. Plate 99 shows a fine example apparently executed by Orchard and probably based on a design by Keller.[10] The realistic representation of small birds among masses of foliage or blossoms, in a manner reminiscent of Far-Eastern art, was greatly in vogue particularly in the eighties (see also Plate 94). A special piece from Stevens & Williams, shown at the International Health Exhibition of London in 1884, conveys in another sense the orientalizing sentiments of the time (Plate 100).

The final flourish of Victorian engraving was the development of 'intaglio' work at Stevens & Williams, mainly by John Northwood, who was art director

---

[6] See James O'Fallon's article in the *Pottery Gazette*, 1885, p. 379, in which he refers specifically to the Baccarat factory.
[7] *English 'Rock Crystal' Glass* (exhibition catalogue), Dudley Art Gallery (1976), p. 8.
[8] Ibid., p. 12.
[9] *Pottery Gazette*, 1884, p. 664. The full title of the exhibition was 'Wolverhampton and Staffordshire Fine Arts and Industrial Exhibition'.
[10] *English 'Rock Crystal' Glass* catalogue (as above), No. 58, plate 15.

96. VASE with 'rock crystal' engraving. Ht. 23.5 cm (9.25 in). Engraved by Frederick E. Kny working at Thomas Webb & Sons, STOURBRIDGE, about 1880. *Victoria and Albert Museum.* *See page 98*

97. DECANTER with 'rock crystal' engraving. Ht. 34.6 cm (13.6 in). Engraved by William Fritsche working at Thomas Webb & Sons, STOURBRIDGE. Probably made in the 1890s. *Formerly in the possession of the makers (Victoria and Albert Museum photograph). See page 98*

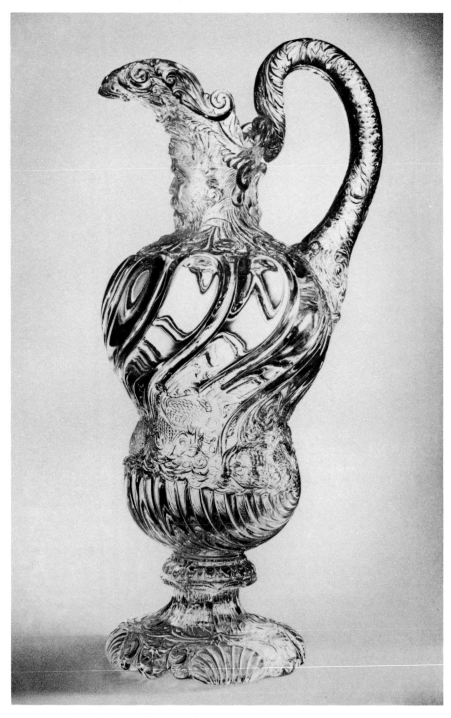

98. JUG with 'rock crystal' engraving. Ht. 38.7 cm (15.25 in). Engraved by
William Fritsche working at Thomas Webb & Sons, STOURBRIDGE; signed
and dated 1886. *The Corning Museum of Glass, New York. See page 98*

99. DECANTER with 'rock crystal' engraving. Ht. 26.4 cm (10.4 in) (no stopper). Engraving apparently executed by John Orchard and probably based on a design by Joseph Keller, at Stevens & Williams, BRIERLEY HILL, 1885. *Dudley Metropolitan Borough (Broadfield House Glass Museum, Kingswinford).* See page 98

100. BOWL with 'rock crystal' engraving. Diam. 27 cm (10.6 in). Designed by John Northwood and engraved by Frank Scheibner for Stevens & Williams, BRIERLEY HILL, 1884. Victoria and Albert Museum. See page 98

from the early eighties until his death in 1902. Midway between cutting and engraving, 'intaglio' can best be considered as deep engraving carried out on wheels which would normally be used for cutting (Plate 101). It gave a distinctive effect whether polished or unpolished, and one of its advantages was that it could be appropriately used in conjunction with normal cut decoration. Besides John Northwood, the name of Joshua Hodgetts is particularly associated with the development of the 'intaglio' technique. It was being worked out about the beginning of the nineties, and by the later nineties intaglio work was an established part of Stevens & Williams' output. It is interesting to notice that the technique was also being used from about this time by American firms such as T. G. Hawkes of Corning, New York.

Acid-etching is a method of engraving which, although distinct in final effect, has usually been related to the process of wheel-engraving. In its simplest form the method consists in covering a glass surface with an acid-resisting substance; the pattern is then cut through the resist, and the whole is dipped in acid, which attacks the surface through the cut-away lines or areas. The commercial application of this principle was entirely a development of the nineteenth century. The Dudley firm of Thomas Hawkes is known to have been producing etched glassware in the thirties. It is said that in 1835 the firm produced an important presentation 'plateau' which was both engraved and etched by William Herbert (see page 86); that a decorator named Denby had perhaps been concerned with etching for Hawkes; and that about 1836 the firm was putting etched decoration on its 'gold enamel' ware (see page 57).[11] Hawkes was presumably followed by other firms in the use of this technique. Early price lists in the possession of Stevens & Williams show that etching was in use for a time by at least one other Midland firm at a period which appears to be about the early forties. These price lists show that etching at the time when they were compiled was by no means confined to flat objects, since the drawings which are inscribed 'etched', or (in one instance) 'etched and engraved', are of vessels such as wineglasses, bottles and vases.

It is clear, however, that in the middle of the century etching was still felt to be in an experimental stage, and that as a method of decoration it was of potential rather than actual commercial value. Benjamin Richardson of the Richardson firm of Stourbridge had begun his career at the Hawkes factory in Dudley, and he may have derived later from that connection some knowledge of etching. In the mid-fifties, when the Richardson firm was under his sole control, he was carrying out further experiments with the process. A blue-layered wineglass, illustrated here, has a deeply etched pattern and is inscribed with Benjamin Richardson's name and the year, 1857, in which he took out a patent for etching in this manner (Plate 102). John Northwood and T. Guest were among those concerned with

---

[11] *Pottery Gazette*, 1882, pp. 68, 255 and 456.

101. WINEGLASS with 'intaglio' floral decoration. Ht. 15.9 cm (6.25 in). Made by
Stevens & Williams, BRIERLEY HILL, about 1900. *Stourbridge Glass
Collection. See page 102*

102. WINEGLASS of layered glass, blue over crystal, with deeply etched decoration; inscribed 'Mr B. Richardson, Wordsley 1857'. Ht. 14.3 cm (5.6 in). *Stourbridge Glass Collection (Victoria and Albert Museum photograph). See page 102*

103. JUG with closely twisted handle, an opaque-white head welded on to the side, and etched decoration. Ht. 22.9 cm (9 in). Etched by J. & J. Northwood, STOURBRIDGE, about 1870. *Stourbridge Glass Collection. See pages 106, 113*

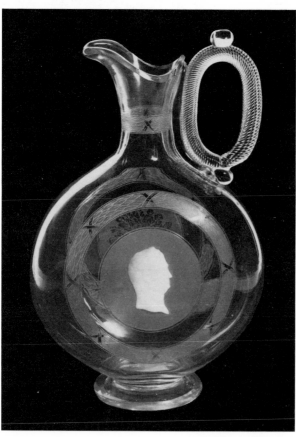

104. Etched VASE. Ht. 21.6 cm (8.5 in). Decorated at the firm of J. & J.
Northwood, STOURBRIDGE. Shown at the Paris exhibition of 1878.
Stourbridge Glass Collection (Victoria and Albert Museum photograph). See page 106

this work at Richardson's; and by the early sixties two important decorating firms specializing in etching, J. & J. Northwood and Guest Brothers, were established in the Stourbridge district. From references to these firms in the pattern books of Thomas Webb's and of Richardson's it seems that they must have been responsible for a great deal of the etching carried out in the district in the later sixties and seventies. Identified examples of J. & J. Northwood's etching have survived through John Northwood's son of the same name (Plates 103, 104), and these include some of the distinguished decorations on fragile and elegant shapes which were shown at the Paris exhibition of 1878.

It will have been noticed that while many of the personalities concerned with conventional and 'rock crystal' engraving in the latter part of the century were Central European immigrants, those responsible for etching and 'intaglio' work in the Midland glass factories were local artists. The same group was also mainly responsible for the cameo glass which seems in retrospect the most remarkable and unexpected product of British glass art in the latter part of the century.

British glassmakers had for long been conscious of the challenge of the Portland vase, the most perfect surviving example of Roman cameo glass, which was in the British Museum.[12] In this context the word 'cameo' implied a vessel made of a dark-coloured glass with an outer layer of opaque-white glass carved away to leave a white pattern in relief against the dark-glass ground. John Northwood was the leading exponent of this exceedingly difficult and tedious technique. After some experimental cameo work he received a commission in 1864 from J. B. Stone (later Sir Benjamin Stone, of the Birmingham glass firm of Stone, Fawdry & Stone), which resulted in the 'Elgin' vase. This piece was finished in 1873 and is now in the Birmingham City Art Gallery. As its name implies, its main decoration is a relief-carved frieze of classical figures; but it cannot be described as cameo work since it is made entirely of clear glass (Plate 105). This was followed by commissions from his cousin Philip Pargeter (at that time the owner of the Red House glassworks near Stourbridge) for a copy of the Portland vase and then for other pieces in the same cameo technique. Among these was the 'Milton' vase, which was decorated with a scene of figures apparently designed by Pargeter himself. In the mid-seventies Thomas Wilkes Webb was also becoming interested in Northwood's work and commissioned from him the 'Pegasus' or 'Dennis' vase, which is now in the Smithsonian Institution in Washington (Plate 106). This was shown in an unfinished state on the Thomas Webb stand at the Paris exhibition of 1878; and at the same exhibition Northwood's 'Milton' vase was to be found on the stand of the James Green firm (known at this time as James Green & Nephew), while his copy of

---

[12] A version of the Portland vase was shown by Richardson's at the 1849 exhibition of the Society of Arts, but it is unlikely that this was seriously imitative in technique. *A Catalogue of Specimens of Recent British Manufactures and Decorative Art . . .*, Society of Arts, London (1849), item 235.

105. The 'Elgin' VASE, of clear glass with etched patterning and a band of relief carving by John Northwood. Ht. 39.4 cm (15.5 in). Commissioned by J. B. (later Sir Benjamin) Stone about 1865 and finished in 1873 (signed, and dated 1873). *City Museum and Art Gallery, Birmingham. See page 106*

106. The 'Pegasus' or 'Dennis' VASE, with cameo decoration by John Northwood. Ht. 54.6 cm (21.5 in). Commissioned by Thomas Wilkes Webb about 1876 and finished in 1882 (signed, and dated 1882). *Smithsonian Institution, Washington. See page 106*

107. Cameo VASE, 'Raising an altar to Bacchus'. Ht. 39.7 cm (15.6 in). Decorated by Alphonse Lechevrel at Hodgetts, Richardson & Son, STOURBRIDGE. Probably shown at the Paris exhibition of 1878. *Brierley Hill Glass Collection.* *See page 111*

108. Cameo VASE. Ht. 21 cm (8.25 in).
Decorated by Charles Northwood
(a nephew of John Northwood) for Stevens
& Williams, BRIERLEY HILL, about
1884. *In the possession of the makers (Victoria and
Albert Museum photograph). See page 111*

109. Cameo PLAQUE, 'Moorish Bathers'.
Diam. 45.7 cm (18 in). Decorated by
George Woodall at Thomas Webb &
Sons, STOURBRIDGE (signed). Begun
about 1890 and finished by 1898. *Private
collection (Victoria and Albert Museum
photograph). See page 111*

the Portland vase was on the stand of the dealer, R. P. Daniell. Cameo work was also being shown at the exhibition by the Richardson firm. This was mainly the work of a French artist, Alphonse Eugène Lechevrel, who was in England for only a few years (Plate 107); but it included also an unfinished version of the Portland vase by Joseph Locke, an artist who had previously been an etcher with Guest Brothers and who was later to continue his career in America.

In the eighties cameo glass was being made on a commercial scale, notably by the two firms of Stevens & Williams and Thomas Webb. This implied the full use of acid etching, and of wheel engraving rather than hand carving for the detailed work. After John Northwood had become art director of Stevens & Williams in the early eighties, the decorating firm of J. & J. Northwood became virtually the cameo workshop for the larger firm. The commercial cameos were naturally based on floral rather than figure subjects, and some of the more unassuming products of this workshop are of considerable beauty (Plate 108). At Thomas Webb's a team of engravers in the cameo workshop was organized under the two brothers Thomas and George Woodall who had been originally with the firm of J. & J. Northwood (Colour Plate F). In the later eighties and nineties George Woodall, in particular, developed a style of figure cameos more personal and more contemporary in spirit than the formal classical manner employed by Northwood. Great virtuosity was shown in making full use of the medium, for instance in graduating the depth of the overlay to indicate distance or the transparency of draperies (Plate 109). At the Chicago exhibition of 1893 the Thomas Webb firm made a feature of prestige work of this sort, and it seems to have been effective in attracting American attention.

Although a little was produced in America and even in Venice,[13] the scope of cameo work in the British style was limited by its costliness. The French glass artist Emile Gallé was working towards the end of the century in a broadly similar medium; but, inspired by a Far-Eastern use of plant motifs in a free flowing style, he produced glasses as different as can be imagined from those of the British cameo artists, whose starting point was classical realism and who delighted in the difficulties of rendering the human form in an intractable material.

---

[13]A. C. Revi, *Nineteenth-Century Glass*, revised edn, New York (1967), pp. 166–72.

4

Later Fancy Glass

The fancy glass of the late nineteenth century was widely based in its appeal, and with its exuberance of form and colour it can perhaps be considered as a revival of the popular spirit in glassware such as was expressed at the beginning of the century in the 'Nailsea' wares (see Chapter 2). The more expensive cut and engraved glass seems in retrospect to have passed through rapid changes of style, but these were slight in comparison with the changes in the fancy glasses, which were often peculiar to individual manufacturers and were altered in appearance quickly and deliberately for the sake of novelty, and also, so it was said, in order to defeat the wiles of foreign copyists.

In some degree all of the fancy glasses reflected the influence of Venetian glass. The appearance of Venetian elements in the middle years of the century has been discussed in an earlier chapter (see page 68). From the time of the London 1862 exhibition the products of Antonio Salviati's revival of earlier Venetian techniques were constantly before the eyes of the manufacturers and the public. It is, however, a surprising fact that in this age, with no inhibitions about copying, exact imitations of Venetian work were rarely attempted for the general market. The reason for this no doubt lay in the very different appearance and characteristics of the British lead-crystal glass as compared with the soda-lime glass of Venice. Glassware incorporating some Venetian techniques of colouring and furnace manipulation was widely made in Europe as elsewhere in the latter half of the century; but in this sort of glassware the British products most closely resembled those of the glass factories of the United States, which were working under similar conditions for very similar markets.

Because the later nineteenth-century fancy glasses were imbued with a spirit of novelty for its own sake their history was inevitably a complicated one. In the sixties and seventies the main interest lay in the formation of a distinctive style of glassware embodying an arbitrary selection of quasi-Venetian elements, and in the development of a novel range of objects for use as table centrepieces. In the eighties the interest shifted to novel variations of the glass material itself and to the production of a bewildering variety of colour techniques. In the nineties elaborate

F. Cameo VASE. Ht. 18.7 cm (7.4 in). Designed by Thomas Woodall, the decoration carried out by J. T. Fereday at Thomas Webb & Sons, STOURBRIDGE, 1884. *Victoria and Albert Museum. See page 111*

G. BOWL of ivory-coloured opaque glass moulded with channels to form an air twist beneath a pale-ruby outer layer, with applied rusticated decoration and satin finish. Ht. 14 cm (5.5 in). Made by Stevens & Williams, BRIERLEY HILL, about 1885. *Stourbridge Glass Collection. See pages 122, 124, 130*

table decorations combined the purpose of the centrepiece with the current fashion for quaint shapes and bizarre colour effects.

Among the Venetian elements which came into fashion was the use of close twists for handles and stems. In the forties and around the middle of the century loose rope-like twists were used, as in the designs of wineglasses registered at the Patent Office Design Registry by J. F. Christy in 1847 and by Richardson's in 1854; but these were relatively uncommon compared with the examples of close twisting, which was popular from the late fifties until the seventies (Plates 103, 110, 117). At the London exhibition of 1862, and again at Paris in 1867, the use of close twisting was a noticeable feature on the stands showing British glass. Of roughly the same period of popularity was the use of small drops or beads usually of opaque coloured glass (Plates 111, 112, 114). Sometimes these were given an impressed shape as 'raspberries', but normally they were left as plain globules attached to the surface of the glass. Used in this way the drops represent a distinctive method of decoration, typical of the sixties and early seventies, which has only a slender connection with Venetian antecedents. Of slightly later incidence was the fashion for close trailing, or threading, which was a speciality of the Richardson firm in the later sixties and seventies. The process was eventually mechanized, with the patenting of glass-threading machines in 1876 by Richardson's and in 1877 by Stevens & Williams (Plates 118, 126). Another such fashion involved the use of ribbing on applied parts such as handles, feet and spouts. About the early sixties little scroll legs came into use, and it was probably as a development of these that the Thomas Webb firm registered in 1867 the design of various ribbed, or 'shell' components. The validity of design registrations lasted only for three years, and by the early seventies the use of ribbing, for handles particularly, was becoming commonplace. In 1870 this device was the subject of further design registrations by the Richardson firm and by another Stourbridge firm, Boulton & Mills, both of which were concerned with registering variations in the nature of the ribbing. Examples are illustrated here from Isaac Barnes of Birmingham and Stevens & Williams, as well as from the Richardson factory (which was called Hodgetts, Richardson & Pargeter in the later sixties and Hodgetts, Richardson & Son from about 1871 to 1882) (Plates 111–14). One of the examples (Plate 113) bears an engraved mark recording the Richardson registration of 1870, although its ribbed handle does not appear to have the alternately broad and narrow ribbing which had been registered on this occasion.

It will be noticed that these decorative adjuncts of the sixties and early seventies were being used mainly on objects of clear uncoloured glass. As yet there was little sign of a serious revival in the use of coloured glass, and the shapes of most of the fancy vessels were still relatively orthodox. Among the other decorative methods used or developed in this period was that of over-all diamond moulding, of which there are many examples in the Thomas Webb pattern books about the

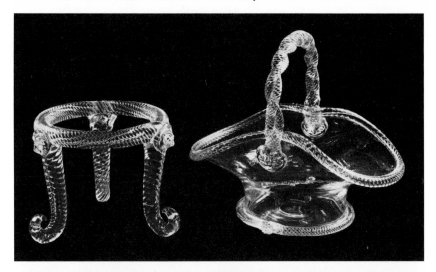

110. Glass BASKET and STAND. Ht. of basket 17.8 cm (7 in). Perhaps made by John Ford, EDINBURGH. The stand resembles ones shown by the Edinburgh firm of John Millar, among others, at the Paris exhibition of 1867. *Janet Paterson loan collection, Huntly House Museum, Edinburgh. See page 113*

111. Covered BOWL and covered VASE decorated with ribbed work and (on the vase) opaque blue drops. Hts 19.1 cm (7.5 in) and 24.1 cm (9.5 in). Made by Isaac Barnes, BIRMINGHAM, about 1870. *City Museum and Art Gallery, Birmingham (Victoria and Albert Museum photograph). See page 113*

112. JUG with ribbed handle, engraved decoration and opaque blue drops. Ht. 12.7 cm (5 in). Made by the Richardson firm, STOURBRIDGE, about 1870–5. *Stourbridge Glass Collection. See page 113*

113. Engraved JUG with ribbed handle. Ht. 14 cm (5.5 in). Made by the Richardson firm, STOURBRIDGE (the base is engraved with registry mark of 1870). *Janet Paterson loan collection, Huntly House Museum, Edinburgh. See page 113*

114. CENTREPIECE, with ribbed arms and acid etched decoration on the bowl and foot. Ht. 38.1 cm (15 in). Made by the Richardson firm, STOURBRIDGE, about 1870–5. *Stourbridge Glass Collection. See page 113*

later fifties; and the practice of waving the edges of bowls and vases, which became suddenly fashionable in the early seventies. The moulding referred to implies the use of a part-size mould to put a slight surface pattern on to glasses which are subsequently free-blown, and should not be confused with full-size moulding whereby glasses are wholly shaped and decorated within the mould (see page 140). Diamond-moulding, and a faint ribbing also produced by mould-blowing, continued to be popular into the latter part of the century (Plate 115). Perhaps the most distinctive of all the resources of fancy glasswork was the well-known Venetian technique of pincered work on heavy trailing. In the form of frills around the necks of vessels this style of decoration first became prominent in the later fifties. In the later sixties the Thomas Webb firm was making a globular decanter with vertical pincered work on the body and stopper, and from the early seventies a great deal of this type of decoration was used by the Richardson firm. A decanter shape associated with pincered trailing was oval in section with a broad flat base, inward sloping sides, either straight or slightly convex, and a narrow frilled neck (Plate 116). Harry J. Powell in his *Glass-making in England* stated that this shape was based on that of a leather bottle and that it was introduced about 1865; but it is noteworthy that similar forms were current in the eighteenth century in Scandinavia and elsewhere on the Continent. A version of this decanter appeared in the Richardson pattern book about 1873, and it was obviously in frequent production in Stourbridge, and elsewhere, towards the end of the century.

The eighteenth-century concept of the epergne survived in some measure into the nineteenth century. An impressive example is shown in Plate 23; but this is to be contrasted with a specifically Victorian mode of table centrepiece which gained popularity in the sixties and lasted into the twentieth century (Plate 130). The success of this sort of glasswork was undoubtedly due to the originality with which it could be used to express a Victorian sense of fantasy. The Victorian centrepieces were capable of taking many forms and of serving many supposed purposes, although always the real function was one of decoration. Sometimes they were described by the eighteenth-century term 'epergnes'. Most often they appear as 'flower stands' or 'flower centres'. When their base took the form of a bowl they might be described as 'fruit and flower glasses'. Sometimes they were partly fitted as candelabra. The London dealers were much concerned with their development; and some of the new ideas may perhaps be traced to Daniel Pearce, who was the junior partner of Dobson & Pearce in the early sixties and of Phillips & Pearce in the later sixties, and who about 1884 took over the department at Thomas Webb's which was concerned with the design and production of this sort of work.

The contemporary use of the term 'flower stand' included the simple combination of a vase and a bowl which was popular for a long period. One of the glasses at the 1851 exhibition shown by the Silesian manufacturer Count

115. Ribbed LIQUEUR DECANTER of colourless glass with blue trailing. Ht. 27.6 cm (10.8 in). Made by James Powell & Sons, LONDON, about 1880–90. *The Museum of London (Victorial and Albert Museum photograph). See page 117*

116. DECANTER with trailed and pincered decoration. Ht. 20.3 cm (8 in). Latter part of the nineteenth century. *Victoria and Albert Museum. See page 117*

Schaffgotsch combined a trumpet-shaped vase and bowl with a circlet of small curved flower holders,[1] and the first item on the Bacchus stand listed in the exhibition catalogue was a 'flower-stand with vase and cornucopias', that is a similar multiple flower stand with a central vase and curved subsidiary flower holders.[2] The first multiple flower stands to appear among the registrations of the British Patent Office Design Registry were those of Dobson & Pearce in June 1861 in the form of a tall trumpet flower vase on a spreading foot with either two or four subsidiary flower holders connected by twisted supports. Flower stands shown at the London exhibition of 1862 included a similarly arranged example by the manufacturers James Powell & Sons, as well as an elaborate confection made by J. (Joseph) Webb & Son of Stourbridge for W. P. & G. Phillips.[3] The possibilities of the multiple flower stands were suddenly apparent and their development was rapid. At the expensive end of the market they were individually designed with great elaboration and for this reason have scarcely ever survived. The development of the more popular forms however can be clearly seen in the design registrations of the sixties and seventies. In April 1862 Dobson & Pearce were registering further examples, including candelabra in a similar style; and later in the same year another firm of London dealers, Naylor & Co., were also beginning to register flower stands. In 1864 and 1865 registrations were made directly by two of the Stourbridge firms—Boulton & Mills and Richardson's. In all these instances the subsidiary flower holders were fixed and nearly all were trumpet shaped, either straight or curved as 'cornucopias'.

Hanging glass 'baskets' had been used in eighteenth-century epergnes; their revival in the nineteenth century seems to have originated in multiple candelabra, an example of which is shown in the illustrations of Powell's glass in the official catalogue of the 1862 exhibition. The first registration of a design for a flower stand with hanging baskets was made by the firm of James Green in March 1866, and within a year the idea was developed in registrations by Richardson's and by J. Dobson. (The Richardson example illustrated in Plate 117 has the baskets of the Richardson registration, but has otherwise almost exactly the same form and arrangement as the James Green registration.) By this time Daniel Pearce had joined W. P. & G. Phillips, and the display of this firm at the Paris exhibition of 1867 brought the original style of flower stands with fixed components for the first time into the illustrated pages of the *Art Journal*; but of more significance was the large chandelier which was also shown at the exhibition and which included an arrangement of hanging baskets. 'Mr Pearce', wrote the *Art Journal* commentator 'is unrivalled in England as a designer of works in glass'. Hanging baskets were

---

[1] *Official Descriptive and Illustrated Catalogue*, vol. III, illustration facing p. 1059, identified as Schaffgotsch from catalogue text.
[2] Ibid., vol. II, p. 699.
[3] J. B. Waring, *Masterpieces . . . at the International Exhibition 1862*, vol. II, plate 116, and vol. I, plate 68.

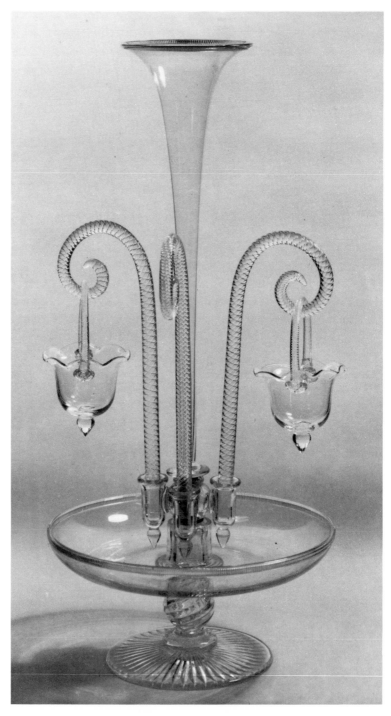

117. FLOWER STAND, originally with four arms each with a hanging basket. Ht. 63.5 cm (25 in). Made by Hodgetts, Richardson & Pargeter, STOURBRIDGE, about 1867. *Stourbridge Glass Collection. See pages 113, 119*

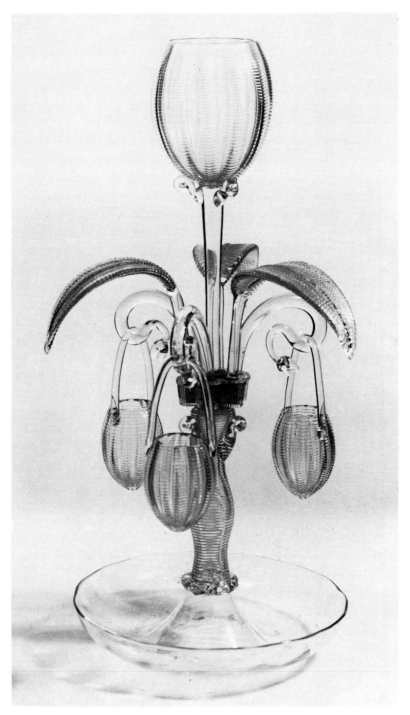

118. FLOWER STAND decorated with ruby trailing. Ht. 63.5 cm (25 in). Made by Hodgetts, Richardson & Son, STOURBRIDGE. The design of the basket is dated 1878. *Stourbridge Glass Collection. See pages 113, 122*

now a normal feature of new registrations for flower stands. One of these, registered by Boulton & Mills in 1871, was also the first registered example of a flower stand mounted on a mirror base or 'plateau', and in 1873 both Philip Pargeter (now separated from the Richardson firm) and Boulton & Mills were registering flower stands of this type decorated with long leaf-shaped components. These so-called 'fern leaves' were a traditional feature of Venetian chandeliers, and they had appeared, for instance, in a Venetian-style chandelier of about 1865 which was made by the Powell firm and is now in the Victoria and Albert Museum. On flower stands the fern leaves were usually placed alternately with the flower holders or the basket supports, as in the 1873 example registered by Pargeter (on the Boulton & Mills example they are arranged in a circle round a solitary central flower vase). A Richardson example of 1878 is shown in Plate 118.

With the flower stands of the seventies the elements of the popular late-Victorian flower stands, with either hanging or fixed flower holders, were already established (Plate 130; see also page 130). Later developments were more transient in their effect, such as some of the relatively expensive flower stands of the eighties, with squat flower holders reminiscent of gaslight shades mounted on plain untwisted arms, and the fashionable random flower stands of the later nineties (see page 130).

The revival of colour became noticeable about the middle of the seventies, and it was immediately associated with a certain freedom, even abandon, of form. Coiled snakes reappeared, and these were followed in the later seventies and in the eighties by a long succession of applied reptiles, fish and flowers, often in the wildest array of colours on bizarre shapes (Plate 119). Among innumerable examples drawn in Thomas Webb's pattern books one particularly grotesque covered vase happens also to be described in words — 'Amber body 4 flint feet 2 puce reptiles on body and 1 on cover Puce flowers Brown leaves'.[4] Some delicate and beautiful effects were, however, achieved with this technique of applied decoration and with the use of acid to produce a 'satin' finish. In the middle eighties Thomas Webb, Stevens & Williams, and probably others too, exploited the current influence from the Far East with pleasing discretion. Two examples illustrated here are from the period when John Northwood was art director at Stevens & Williams, and are typical of a large class of such bowls with crimped rims and applied decoration of leaves or flowers (Colour Plate G and Plate 120).

The eighties and nineties were the two decades during which the glass manufacturers were most deeply concerned with the production of fancy glass novelties. In the eighties most of the named novelties were in effect new methods of colouring, figuring or otherwise decorating the glass material itself. Some glasses shaded imperceptibly from one colour to another; some were made to

---

[4] No. 12807.

119. BOWL of opalescent glass with silver leaf decoration and applied amber-coloured fish. Ht. 10.2 cm (4 in). About 1880–5. *Stourbridge Glass Collection.* *See page 122*

120. VASE of pale-blue glass with applied uncoloured glass 'acanthus' leaves and satin finish. Ht. 10.2 cm (4 in). Made by Stevens & Williams, BRIERLEY HILL, about 1883. *Stourbridge Glass Collection. See page 122*

123

imitate carved ivory; some had embedded white or coloured canes in the manner of Venetian 'latticino' decoration, or had coloured glasses trailed upon them and combed in the manner of slipware pottery. This sort of activity can be said to have begun with some iridescent glasses which appeared in the seventies, followed by the great success of Thomas Webb's iridescent 'Bronze' glass at the Paris exhibition of 1878. Thereafter a remarkable series of fancy glasses came from this factory—such as 'Peach' (1885), 'Burmese' (1886), 'Old Roman' (1888) and 'Tricolor' (1889)—together with many others from Midland factories, not all of which are easily identified among surviving examples. The best known of these novelties was undoubtedly Thomas Webb's 'Burmese' (or, more fully, 'Queen's Burmese Ware'), which was an almost opaque greenish-yellow glass shaded under heat treatment to a deep pink (Plate 121). This glass was much used for the patent 'fairy lights', or small individual candle shades, which enjoyed a great vogue in this country, as also in America, in the later eighties. The popularity of 'Burmese' emphasizes the close connection between the glasses of Britain and America during this phase, for it was originally a novelty of the Mount Washington Glass Company of New Bedford, Massachusetts.

Among the technical developments of the period was a method of trapping air in moulded recesses between an opaque glass body and a tinted outer layer. This method was used to produce the linear decoration on the Stevens & Williams bowl on Colour Plate G. It was used most frequently, in this country and in America, with an over-all diamond mould under the overlay, which was also finished to give a slightly matt satin surface (Plate 122). As an added show of virtuosity this so-called satin glass might even have a further overlay in a contrasting colour etched away to leave sprays of flowers in relief (Plate 123). Another luxury product of the period was the painted and gilded glass, such as came from the workshop established at Thomas Webb's under the French artist Jules Barbe (Plates 124, 125). In the later eighties much of Barbe's work was concerned with the decoration of 'Burmese' ware. At Stevens & Williams enamel-painting, and similar work such as decoration by a deposit of silver on the glass surface, was carried out by another Frenchman, named Oscar Pierre Erard (Plates 126, 127). A further sign of French influence may perhaps be discerned in the appearance at Stevens & Williams and elsewhere of the attractive fancy glass called 'moss agate', which with its interior crackle and colour streaking is reminiscent of the effects achieved by the French glass artist Eugène Rousseau (Plate 128).

In the later eighties and in the nineties the names applied to novelties in the *Pottery Gazette* and in makers' pattern books often refer not to the colour or figuring of the glass material but to specific styles of glass decorations for the table or sideboard. As in the instance of 'Rusticana', produced by John Walsh Walsh of Birmingham in 1896, the novelty might consist in a number of devices of related design for holding plant pots. More usually the purpose of these table

121. Two VASES of semi-opaque shaded 'Burmese' glass. Hts. 15.2 cm (6 in) and 6.3 cm (2.5 in). Made by Thomas Webb & Sons, STOURBRIDGE, about 1890. *Stourbridge Glass Collection. See page 124*

122. BOWL of white opaque glass moulded to form a diamond air-lock pattern beneath an outer layer of multicoloured glass, with rusticated feet and satin finish. Ht. 12.7 cm (5 in). Made by Stevens & Williams, BRIERLEY HILL, in the later 1880s. *Stourbridge Glass Collection. See page 124*

123. VASE with a diamond air-lock pattern between opaque and translucent layers, covered by an outer layer etched away to form a floral pattern in relief and with satin finish. Ht. 26 cm (10.25 in). Made by Thomas Webb & Sons, STOURBRIDGE, probably in the early 1890s (marked 'Webb Pat. 1889'). *Mr A. Christian Revi. See page 124*

124. Opaque glass VASE, painted and
gilded. Ht. 30.5 cm (12 in). Made
by Thomas Webb & Sons,
STOURBRIDGE (marked), and
presumably decorated by Jules
Barbe. About 1890. *Mr A.
Christian Revi. See page 124*

125. Gilded VASE. Ht. 24.8 cm
(9.75 in). Decorated by Jules Barbe
at Thomas Webb & Sons,
STOURBRIDGE, probably about
1890. *Brierley Hill Glass Collection.
See page 124*

126. VASE with painted decoration covered by close trailing ('Tapestry' glass). Ht. 21.6 cm (8.5 in). Made by Stevens & Williams, BRIERLEY HILL, and decorated by Oscar Pierre Erard. The design is dated 1892. *In the possession of the makers. See pages 113, 124*

H. DECANTER of green glass. Ht. 26.3 cm (10.4 in). Designed by the architect
T. G. Jackson (later Sir Thomas Graham Jackson, Bt.) for James Powell &
Sons, LONDON, in 1874. *Victoria and Albert Museum. See page 133*

I. Pressed glass VASE of deep-purple glass. Ht. 14.3 cm (5.6 in). Made by John Derbyshire, SALFORD, with marks both of the manufacturer and of registration in 1876. *Victoria and Albert Museum. See page 159*

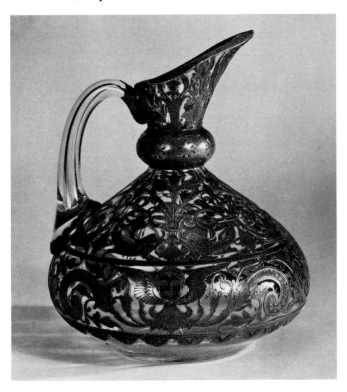

127. JUG with engraved silver deposit. Ht. 14.6 cm (5.75 in). Made by Stevens & Williams, BRIERLEY HILL, and decorated by Oscar Pierre Erard. The design is dated 1886. *In the possession of the makers (Victoria and Albert Museum photograph).* See page 124

128. VASE with crackled and colour-streaked body ('moss agate' glass). Ht. 14.6 cm (5.75 in). Made by Stevens & Williams, BRIERLEY HILL, about 1888. *In the possession of the makers Victoria and Albert Museum photograph).* See page 124

129

decorations, if they were to have a purpose at all, was to hold flowers. This was the period when rusticated work was greatly in vogue, and most of the fancy glass of this sort made use of rusticated feet and supports if it was not wholly in the form of tree trunks and roots (Plate 129). A novelty would normally consist of a number of variations on a basic design, such as flower holders in the form of foxglove flowers mounted on rusticated stems (John Walsh Walsh, 1898), or groupings of hollow glass bamboo sticks (Richardson, 1899). A series could thus include a considerable number of matching pieces, with vertical and horizontal arrangements, varying perhaps from a piece with a solitary flower holder to a large one with many holders which would form a table centrepiece. It is noteworthy that these table decorations, which were unfettered by precedents in glass design, expressed very clearly the end-of-century feeling for plant forms and asymmetrical arrangements.

The same tendencies can be seen in the many flower stands of the later nineties in which asymmetrical arrangements of glass flower holders were supported on thin metal stands; in the tall vases with vegetable-like lobes and swelling bases which seem to have been a speciality of Stevens & Williams in the same period; and in the waved edges which were widely used on the fancy wares. Waved edging had been in vogue since the early seventies, and had developed into both tight and loose varieties which could be used together (Colour Plate G); but in the nineties the waving often imparted to glasses a strikingly flower-like shape (Plate 137), especially in the extreme case of the rims with one side turned vertically up and the other down.

Probably the most popular hand-made glass at the latter end of the century, in the sense that it reached the least sophisticated market, was a type of ruby-coloured ware decorated in a somewhat old-fashioned manner with handles, feet, knobs, frillings and pincered trailings of clear untinted glass. The appearance of pincered trailing in the late fifties has already been mentioned (see page 117), and subsequently this style of decoration was increasingly associated with cheap ruby glass. A lot of it was made in the factories of the Stourbridge district, but it was also the typical product of the small back-yard 'cribs' which were operating in the Midlands around the end of the nineteenth century and into the first decade or so of the twentieth century. Presumably these small establishments found the production of ruby convenient, since in some degree the colour masked the poor quality of their material, which was derived from the remelting of waste glass. An elaborate ruby flower stand, illustrated here, is by a known maker working in these circumstances in the early twentieth century (Plate 130). Cribs of this sort are also known to have produced many of the surviving friggers such as fancy glass pipes and walking sticks (see page 53).[5]

---

[5]Sir Hugh Chance, *Trans. Worcestershire Archaeological Society for 1959*, XXXVI, p. 42, et seq.

129. FLOWER HOLDER of topaz opalescent glass. Ht. 25.4 cm (10 in). About
1895. *Stourbridge Glass Collection. See page 130*

130. FLOWER STAND of ruby and clear glass. Ht. 57.2 cm (22.5 in). Made by
George Ernest Fox in the BROMSGROVE district, 1900–22. *Sir Hugh Chance.*
See pages 117, 122, 130

At the opposite pole of glasswork, the most sophisticated and self-conscious productions of the latter part of the nineteenth century were also based on the methods of Venetian glass and for this reason had much in common with the popular fancy wares. Reference has already been made to an intellectual antipathy to cut glass (see page 37), and in some degree this can also be taken to include engraved glass. The first glass associated with the Arts and Crafts movement was designed for William Morris by the architect Philip Webb and made by the London firm of James Powell & Sons. Glassware on a sheet of designs by Philip Webb, preserved in the Victoria and Albert Museum, is inscribed as intended for William Morris, with the date January 1860. Plate 131 illustrates two examples from a group of Philip Webb's glasses with horizontal bulges and a somewhat Gothic cast of design which were made by James Powell & Sons and apparently sold by Morris's firm Morris, Marshall, Faulkner & Co. from the early sixties onwards. In 1874 another table-set in a similar but more delicate style was designed for Powell's by another architect, T. G. Jackson, later Sir Thomas Graham Jackson, Bt. (Colour Plate H). Henceforth this firm, which by the latter part of the century was the last surviving London manufacturer of hand-made glass, tended increasingly to represent an intellectual and purist attitude towards glassmaking. It was not quite alone in this, however, for other firms also seem to have taken up this role from time to time in some productions. The Edinburgh firm of A. Jenkinson was noticed at the Paris exhibition of 1878 for its speciality in the very thin and delicately blown style of glassware known as 'muslin' or 'mousseline' glass.[6] In the eighties, and later, James Couper & Sons of Glasgow were using a deliberately bubbled and streaked material for their 'Clutha' glasses, which they were so proud to have had designed by the well-known designer Christopher Dresser that they had the fact etched on the base of every piece (Plate 132). This glass was closely matched by Thomas Webb's 'Old Roman', and in 1888 the Glasgow firm were complaining that the latter was a deliberate imitation of 'Clutha'.[7] In a later phase, about 1896, more 'Clutha' glasses were designed by the Glasgow designer George Walton, and some of these were varied with patches of aventurine in the glass material (Plate 133). Christopher Dresser was also responsible for some strikingly 'functional' wares combining glass and silver, such as the example illustrated in Plate 134 which was registered in 1879 by the Birmingham silversmiths Hukin & Heath.

The most distinctive work from the Powell factory involved the use of furnace-manipulated decoration on lightly tinted vessels. Two examples are illustrated here from a group of glasses acquired by the Victoria and Albert Museum in 1877; one is made of opalescent glass, and both are Venetian in form (Plates 135, 136). A later example also makes use of the opalescent glass (Plate 137). An

[6]*Magazine of Art*, 1878–9, p. 98.
[7]*Pottery Gazette*, 1888, p. 1115.

131. Two GLASSES. Hts. 9.5 cm (3.75 in) and 12.7 cm (5 in). From a set designed by Philip Webb, probably in the early 1860s, and made by James Powell & Sons, LONDON. *Victoria and Albert Museum. See page 133*

132. Two VASES of green bubbled and streaked glass ('Clutha' glass). Hts. 12.7 cm (5 in) and 7.6 cm (3 in). Designed by Christopher Dresser for James Couper & Sons, GLASGOW (marked), in the later 1880s. *Victoria and Albert Museum. See page 133*

133. VASE and BOWL of green bubbled and streaked glass, the bowl also with aventurine patches ('Clutha' glass). Hts. 14 cm (5.5 in) and 7.7 cm (3 in). Designed by George Walton for James Couper & Sons, GLASGOW, about 1896. *Victoria and Albert Museum. See page 133*

134. CLARET JUG mounted in silver. Ht. 24.8 cm (9.75 in). Designed by Christopher Dresser and registered in 1879 by the Birmingham silversmiths Hukin & Heath. *Victoria and Albert Museum. See page 133*

135. GOBLET of opalescent glass. Ht. 21.9 cm (8.6 in). Made by James Powell & Sons, LONDON, 1876. *Victoria and Albert Museum.* *See page 133*

136. STANDING BOWL of green glass with colourless glass handles. Ht. 11.4 cm (4.5 in). Made by James Powell & Sons, LONDON, 1876. *Victoria and Albert Museum.* *See page 133*

 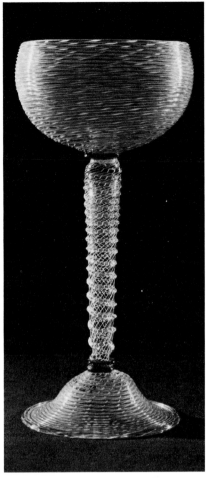

137. VASE of tinted opalescent glass. Ht. 22.2 cm (8.75 in). Made by James Powell & Sons, LONDON. The style was current in the 1890s. *The Museum of London (Victoria and Albert Museum photograph). See pages 130, 133*

138. GOBLET of blue-green glass striped with white and covered with trailing. Ht. 21.6 cm (8.5 in). Prize object from the Society of Arts' competition of 1869–70, made by Joseph Leicester at James Powell & Sons, LONDON. *Victoria and Albert Museum. See page 139*

139. GOBLET of clear glass with applied decoration in green. Ht. 20.6 cm (8.1 in) Made by James Powell & Sons, LONDON, about 1895–1900. *The Museum of London (Victoria and Albert Museum photograph). See page 139*

140, 141. Two tinted GLASSES with trailed decoration. Hts. (a) 27.9 cm (11 in), (b) 19.1 cm (7.5 in). Made by James Powell & Sons, LONDON, and bought in Paris in 1900. *Nordenfjeldske Kunstindustrimuseum, Trondheim. See page 139*

interesting sidelight upon the style and outlook of the firm is provided by the career of Joseph Leicester, the craftsman who with a remarkably expert entry won a Society of Arts prize in 1869–70 (Plate 138). He was later a Member of Parliament for many years; but whilst he was an employee at Powell's he was sent by the Society of Arts to the Paris exhibitions of 1867 and 1878, and his report on the latter occasion shows very well the regard of his firm for simple dignified glasswork with furnace ornamentation.[8] From about 1880 the firm's productions were under the direct control of Harry J. Powell, who remained active until the time of the First World War and came to be regarded as one of the most distinguished of modern glass artists. Much of his work in the latter part of the nineteenth century was in deliberate imitation of the glasswork of other periods, and for this purpose he used soda-lime glass as well as lead crystal. Glasses seen in Old Master paintings and in museums were fertile sources of inspiration, and sometimes ideas from diverse sources were combined to produce unusual and interesting effects (Plate 139). At the very end of the century he was designing glasses of an original quality which made a worthy contribution to the international 'Art Nouveau' style (Plates 140, 141).

[8] *The Society of Arts Artisan Reports on the Paris Universal Exhibition of 1878,* London (1879), p. 109, et seq.

5

Mould-Blown and Press-Moulded Glass

One of the main achievements of nineteenth-century glass technology was the development of mechanical means of producing glassware with relief decoration. The use of moulds, to determine shape and pattern, is as old as Roman glass; but it was only with the nineteenth century that the techniques of moulding were systematically developed as a means of producing cheaply decorated table and ornamental glass. They were developed also as a means of making bottles, ultimately by automatic methods, but the processes of commercial bottle making are necessarily beyond the limits of this review.

In the years about the beginning of the century the traditional method of blowing glass into a one-piece part-size mould was often used to impart flutes to the lower part of a decanter or jug which was otherwise to be decorated with cutting. The method of shaping and patterning an object wholly by blowing the molten glass into a full-size two- or three-piece mould was a means of producing fancy bottles and similar wares; but it does not seem to have been used for table wares in Britain to the same extent as in the United States of America around the twenties and thirties, where the 'blown-three-mould' glass was produced in quantity, and has been widely studied. When a relief pattern is got by the simple process of blowing a vessel in a mould, a ghost of the pattern appears in reverse on the inner surface, matching convexity with concavity. Normally the outer pattern made by this method is a little blurred and smooth to the touch, but a considerable degree of sharpness could be got by using mechanical methods of blowing. An adaptation of mould-blowing, and one which was suited to large-scale patterns, was known as 'pillar moulding'. Apsley Pellatt, writing in the late forties, described this as a recent introduction (apart from the fact that it seemed to have been used by the Romans).[1] It consisted in blowing into a part-size mould a relatively cool gather of molten glass which had been given an outer coating of fully molten glass. Heavily protrusive pillars could thus be moulded on the out-side of a glass vessel without affecting the regularity of the inside surface (Plate 142).

---

[1] *Curiosities of Glass Making*, London (1849), p. 104, et seq.

142. BOWL, decorated with 'pillar moulding'. Ht. 9 cm (3.5 in). Made by Apsley Pellatt, LONDON, 1851. *Photograph by the Musée des Techniques, Conservatoire National des Arts et Métiers, Paris. See page 140*

143. Cut-glass TOILET-WATER BOTTLE with intaglio moulded head of Queen Adelaide, marked 'Adelaide' and 'Pellatt & Co. Patentees'. Ht. 10.5 cm (4.1 in). Made by Pellatt & Co. (Apsley Pellatt), LONDON, in accordance with a patent taken out in 1831. *Museum and Art Gallery, Worthing.* *See page 142*

A decade or so earlier Apsley Pellatt had used a curious method of producing finely modelled patterns on mould-blown wares. This was the subject of the first part of a patent which he took out in 1831 and which is described in the patent documents. A cake of 'earthy composition', impressed with the desired pattern, was placed in a segment of the mould; the cake adhered to the glass object blown in the mould, and was not removed until after the object had been finished and annealed. The method was practical, and gave a deep and detailed impression. It was used for somewhat the same purpose as Pellatt used the sulphides, to provide, for instance, an intaglio bust of Queen Adelaide on a scent bottle decorated with fine cutting; but such work is unusual, and it was presumably not a commercial success (Plate 143).

Besides its use for commercial bottle making, mould-blowing continued to be one of the well-known resources of glassmaking; but from the time of its introduction the new process of press-moulding attracted the main attention of those who were concerned with the production of cheaply decorated wares, since a sharp relief pattern could be obtained on the outer surface of a vessel while the inner surface retained a regular contour and was not broken by hollows and ridges. The method was to press a controlled quantity of molten glass between a mould and a plunger, the mould being a negative of the outer surface of the vessel and the plunger a negative of the inner surface. The process could only be used to form open shapes from which the plunger could be withdrawn, but some degree of manipulation might be subsequently used to change the outline of a pressed vessel, and a vessel might be made of separately pressed parts. The glass surface resulting from contact with the metal mould was somewhat rough, but this was later corrected by a process of heat treatment, known as 'fire polishing'.

A primitive sort of press-moulding had been used at the end of the eighteenth century for the solid bases of cut-glass salad bowls and goblets; but the technique of pressing hollow wares was apparently an American invention of the middle twenties. It was soon being used in this country and elsewhere in Europe; and in 1831 Apsley Pellatt included a drawing of the 'machine for pressing glass by the mode lately introduced from America' in the documents relating to the second part of the patent he took out in that year (which was concerned not with pressing as such, but with a method of assembling moulds). Most of the early British pressed glass, however, was made in the Midlands. In Birmingham Rice Harris & Son and Bacchus & Green (known as Bacchus, Green & Green before about 1834 and George Bacchus & Sons after about 1840); in Dudley Thomas Hawkes; and in Stourbridge the Richardson firm (Webb & Richardson until 1836) and Wheeley & Davis (the predecessors of Davis, Greathead & Green) are all mentioned as early manufacturers.[2] At the Birmingham exhibition of 1849 pressed glass was shown by Rice Harris, by Bacchus and by Lloyd &

[2]*Pottery Gazette*, 1881, p. 1061; 1883, p. 1139; 1885, p. 903; 1888, pp. 50, 912.

Summerfield. By this time pressed glass was being widely made, but at the 1851 exhibition Rice Harris was the only leading manufacturer whose pressed glass was mentioned in the catalogues.

Most of the American pressed glass of the thirties and early forties was decorated in the 'lacy' style, which implies that freely conceived relief patterns were surrounded by finely stippled, or matted, grounds. Broadly similar work is known to have been produced in France, Belgium and Sweden during the decade or so before the middle of the century. It is unfortunate that no early pattern books or catalogues are known which would indicate precisely the patterns used by the early pressed-glass manufacturers in Britain. We can assume that pieces commemorating British royal events are of British origin and that they were designed at the time of the events with which they are associated. This would apply to pieces commemorating the accession and coronation of Queen Victoria in 1837 and 1838, her wedding in 1839 and the creation of her infant son as Prince of Wales in 1841 (Plates 144–7). Some of the commemorative pieces are found to have letters incorporated in the pattern and these are assumed to be the marks of independent die-sinkers who produced the moulds. Of those illustrated here one has the letters 'WR', another the letter 'D' and a third the letter 'W'. Directories of the period show that Birmingham had become the principal centre of die-sinking in the thirties. All the letters in question could be matched from the names of the die-sinkers there, but in particular the letter combination 'WR' may represent William Reading, whose name appears at intervals as an independent operator among the Birmingham die-sinkers from 1828 onwards. The letters 'WR' appear on a number of other patterns in the international 'lacy' style. In the example illustrated on Plate 148 they even appear exceptionally on a well-known pattern which is associated with the French factory of Baccarat, and which is included also in the catalogues of the Belgian factory of Val St. Lambert.[3] One can only speculate as to whether in these instances die-sinkers would be acting as free-lance purveyors of moulds, original or copied, or acting at the behest of particular manufacturers. The importance of the die-sinkers in the early manufacture of pressed glass is illustrated by references in articles in the *Pottery Gazette*, written in the eighties, to a Birmingham die-sinker named James Stevens, who performed the difficult feat of making the first mould for a pressed tumbler in the mid-thirties; this is identified as a fluted tumbler and was subsequently put into production by Rice Harris. It was said that James Stevens had previously made moulds for pressed-glass salts for the United States, as well as similar vessels for Rice Harris.[4]

---

[3] The pattern is identical, apart from the central star, with the Baccarat design in a Launay Hautin catalogue of about 1842 illustrated in Elisa Steenberg, *Svenskt Adertonhundratals Glas*, plate 11; and it is apparently identical with a design in Vale St. Lambert catalogues of 1843 and 1847. See also Ruth Webb Lee, *Sandwich Glass*, 2nd edn., Framlingham Centre, Mass. (1939), p. 401, plate 162.

[4] *Pottery Gazette*, 1885, p. 903; 1888, p. 815; 1894, p. 604.

144. Pressed glass PLATE with head of Queen Victoria and 'VR' (Victoria Regina), probably in commemoration of her accession in 1837. The letter 'D' occurs in the border pattern near the lower edge. Diam. 11.4 cm (4.5 in). *Mr and Mrs Charles Benson. See pages 143, 147*

145. Pressed glass PLATE with the royal crown and 'VR' (Victoria Regina), probably in commemoration of Queen Victoria's coronation in 1838. The letters 'WR' occur in the border near the upper edge of the plate. Diam. 12.7 cm (5 in). *Private Collection (Victoria and Albert Museum photograph). See page 143*

146. Pressed PLATE, of amber-coloured glass, with busts of Queen Victoria and Prince Albert, probably commemorating the royal marriage of 1839. The letter 'W' occurs beneath the representation of the Queen. Diam. 12.7 cm (5 in). *Private collection. See page 143*

147. Pressed glass PLATE with the insignia of the Prince of Wales, probably commemorating the creation of the infant Edward as Prince of Wales in 1841. Diam. 12.4 cm (4.9 in). *Mr and Mrs Charles Benson. See page 143*

148. Pressed glass PLATE, with initials 'WR' incorporated in the border pattern (beneath the arabesque at the top of the photograph). Diam. 26.5 cm (10.5 in). The design is associated with the French factory of Baccarat and also with the Belgian factory of Val St. Lambert. *Mrs Mary K. Bishop (Victoria and Albert Museum photograph). See page 143*

Clearly the British manufacturers were involved in the international manifestation of lacy glass, especially in the use of raised scroll patterns in the current Second Rococo style. It may be suspected, however, that from the beginning they were showing more interest than those elsewhere in the use of patterns derived from cut glass. One of the early commemorative pieces illustrated here is decorated in this manner (Plate 144). A *Pottery Gazette* writer in the eighties specifically stated that the first of the pressed-glass dishes were pillared in pattern, that is, they were decorated with pillared flutes;[5] and it is significant that the first registrations of pressed-glass designs at the Patent Office Design Registry, which were made in 1840 by the Birmingham firms of Rice Harris and John Gold, were almost entirely for cut-glass patterns in the broad-fluted style (see page 29). The attraction of such patterns would be obvious in a country where real cut glass was familiar, although too expensive for everyday use by the majority of the population.

By the middle of the century further illustrations of the imitation of cut glass were appearing in the pages of the *Art Journal* and the *Journal of Design and Manufactures*.[6] The designs were mainly based still on broad-flute cutting, with the slight belatedness that was to be expected of imitative work. Some seem to show the common tendency of pressed glass to use cut patterns in a manner which would be inappropriate or unduly expensive if the decoration were truly cut. A fruit dish of this nature, believed to be by Bacchus, is illustrated on Plate 149.[7] There was obviously a great output of tumblers, which were relatively broad and squat; the example illustrated in Plate 150 can be taken as typical of those being designed and made around the middle of the century. In the fifties some of the patterns reflected the mid-century use of large motifs in cut glass, as in the instance of a pattern illustrated here which was registered by Robinson & Bolton of Warrington in 1856 (Plate 151). A tendency of the later fifties and early sixties, as exemplified by the many registrations of the Joseph Webb factory of Stourbridge, was to make pressed-glass objects as though they were decorated by rows of cut hollows; but this unobtrusive form of contemporary cutting became altogether more cumbersome when translated into pressed glass. The spirit of contemporary cut glass was perhaps reflected most exactly in a design, registered by the Tutbury Glass Company in 1864, which consisted of an over-all pattern of comparatively small and widely spaced stars.

The copying of unobtrusive patterns was one result of the eclipse of cut glass around the sixties (see page 37), but this period saw also a number of developments in pressed-glass design which had little or no connection with the technique of cutting. Although cut motifs were still used, and always have been

[5]Ibid., 1887, p. 1075.
[6]*Art Journal*, 1849, p. 307; *Journal of Design and Manufactures*, vol. III (1850), pp. 16 and 17.
[7]A broadly similar design by Bacchus is illustrated in *Journal of Design and Manufactures*, vol. IV (1850–1), p. 94.

149. Pressed glass FRUIT DISH. Ht. 18.4 cm (7.25 in). Probably made by George Bacchus & Sons, BIRMINGHAM, about 1850. *Victoria and Albert Museum.*
See page 147

150. Pressed TUMBLER. Ht. 10.2 cm (4 in). About 1850. *Victoria and Albert Museum. See page 147*

151. Pressed SUGAR BOWL and MILK JUG with applied wrought handle. Hts. 16.5 cm (6.5 in) and 14.6 cm (5.75 in). Made by Robinson & Bolton, WARRINGTON, from a pattern registered in 1856 (the jug bears a registry mark). *Bradford Art Galleries and Museums (Cliffe Castle, Keighley). See page 147*

used, the manufacturers began to explore the various effects which were especially appropriate to pressed glass. Perhaps as a result of the use of widely spaced motifs, it was noticed that the impressed patterns appeared more emphatic if the surrounding surface of the glass were roughened. This simple method of obtaining a contrast in surface texture was probably used by the Tutbury Company for their star pattern mentioned above; and it was used a good deal by the Manchester firm of Molineaux, Webb & Co., often with attractive results (Plate 152). Among the first of the glasses of this sort registered by Molineaux, Webb were a number decorated with the Greek key pattern; and these, appearing from 1864 onwards, may be considered as reflections of the current enthusiasm for engraving and acid etching. They were followed at a later date by other makers using naturalistic designs. Vine patterns are illustrated here from the firm of Henry Greener, Sunderland, in 1876, and from Sowerby's Ellison glassworks, Gateshead, in 1887 (Plates 153, 154). Three-dimensional imitative forms might also be used, as in several instances of vessels in the form of a swan or human hands (Plate 155). In a similar manner vessels might be conceived as miniature models of familiar objects, such as a boat registered by Hodgetts, Richardson & Son in 1872, a 'Lady's Boot' registered by John Derbyshire of Salford in 1875 or a coal wagon registered by W. H. Heppell of Newcastle upon Tyne in 1880 (Plate 156). Sculptural glass objects were also being produced in a manner which recalled the glass busts of the mid-century years (see page 74). In one year, 1874, John Derbyshire registered a lion (Plate 157), a greyhound and a Britannia figure, followed in 1876 by a winged sphinx. In this phase of the history of pressed glass the British firms were clearly acting in close connection with the equivalent firms in the United States, although the details of their interaction have still to be worked out. It is of interest to notice that two of the designs illustrated here, registered in 1876 (Plates 153, 155), were preceded by similar designs patented in the United States in 1870 and 1875 respectively.[8]

One of the features of pressed-glass design in the seventies and eighties was the use of raised dots and stippled grounds, in a style which recalls the 'lacy' glass of the thirties. Edgings and border patterns formed by single rows of large raised dots appeared in the Molineaux, Webb design-registrations of the mid-sixties, and also in Sowerby designs of the late sixties and early seventies. Probably the first British registered design using a stippled ground of small raised dots was one registered by Henry Greener in 1869 with the inscription 'Gladstone for the million' (Plate 158). In this instance the lettering of the name was decorated with large dots, and a similar convention was used to commemorate other notabilities and for the lettered ware produced for Queen Victoria's Jubilee in 1887 (Plate 159).

As might be expected, designs for pressed or other moulded glass reflected the

---

[8]I am indebted for this information to Mr A. Christian Revi.

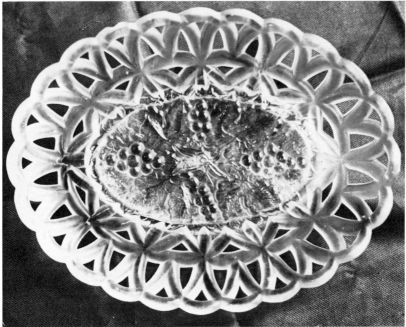

152. STANDING DISH, pressed and with outer surface partly roughened. Ht. 13 cm (5.1 in). Made by Molineaux, Webb & Co., MANCHESTER, and dated (by registry mark) 1868. *Author's collection. See page 150*

153. Pressed DISH, partly with satin finish. Length 28.3 cm (11.1 in). Made by Henry Greener, SUNDERLAND, and dated (by registry mark) 1876. A similar design was patented in the United States by Hobbs, Brockunier & Co., Wheeling, West Virginia, in 1870. *Gray Art Gallery and Museum, Hartlepool. See page 150*

154. Pressed MUG. Ht. 8.9 cm (3.5 in). Made by Sowerby, GATESHEAD, and marked with serial number of registration in 1887. *Author's collection.* *See page 150*

155. DISH in the form of two hands, with satin finish. Length 19 cm (7.5 in). The design was registered by John Ford, EDINBURGH, in 1876, having been previously patented in the United States in 1875 for W. L. Libbey & Son, East Cambridge, Mass. *Gray Art Gallery and Museum, Hartlepool. See page 150*

156. Pressed BOWL in the form of a coal wagon. Ht. 8.9 cm (3.5 in). Made by
W. H. Heppell, NEWCASTLE UPON TYNE, and dated (by registry mark)
1880. *Kirklees Museums Service (Tolson Memorial Museum, Huddersfield).*
See page 150

157. Pressed glass PAPERWEIGHT with satin finish, in the form of a lion 'after
Landseer'. Ht. 12.1 cm (4.75 in). Made by John Derbyshire, SALFORD. The
piece bears both the manufacturer's mark and the mark of registration in 1874.
Victoria and Albert Museum. See page 150

158. Pressed SUGAR BOWL, with inscription 'Gladstone for the million'.
Ht. 11.7 cm (4.6 in). Made by Henry Greener, SUNDERLAND, and dated
(by registry mark) 1869. *Author's collection. See page 150*

159. Pressed DISH. Diam. 24.1 cm (9.5 in). Made by Matthew Turnbull,
SUNDERLAND, 1887. *Tyne and Wear County Council Museums (Sunderland
Museum). See page 150*

160. Pressed VASE of opalescent glass. Ht. 14.9 cm (5.9 in). Made by Sowerby, GATESHEAD (marked). The pattern was registered in 1877, and the piece bears the registry mark. *Tyne and Wear County Council Museums (Shipley Art Gallery, Gateshead).* See page 159

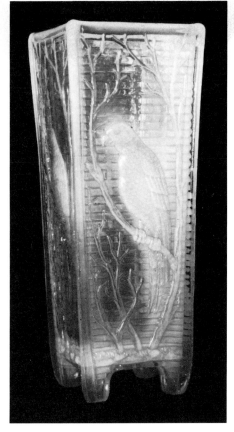

161. Pressed BOWL of clear glass. Ht. 7 cm (2.75 in). Made by Sowerby, GATESHEAD (marked). The form, but not the floral detail, was registered in 1881, and the piece bears the registry mark. *Tyne and Wear County Council Museums (Shipley Art Gallery, Gateshead).* See page 159

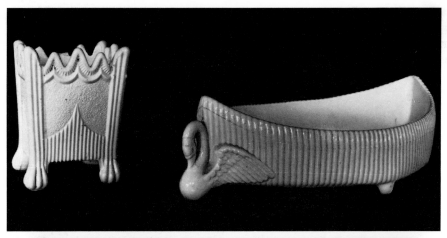

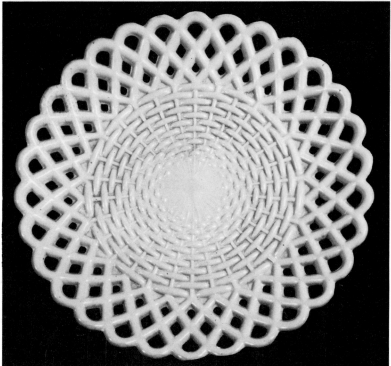

162. Pressed VASE and BOWL of turquoise-blue and cream-coloured opaque glasses. Hts. 8.9 cm (3.5 in) and 6 cm (2.4 in). Made by Sowerby, GATESHEAD (both marked). The patterns were registered in 1877 and 1878 (the second without the flutes), and both pieces bear registry marks. *Tyne and Wear County Council Museums (Shipley Art Gallery, Gateshead). See page 159*

163. Pressed DISH of blue opaque glass. Diam. 22.2 cm (8.75 in). Made by Sowerby, GATESHEAD, probably about 1880. *Tyne and Wear County Council Museums (Shipley Art Gallery, Gateshead). See page 159*

164. Moulded BOWL and VASE of opaque marbled glasses ('slag glass').
Hts. 5.1 cm (2 in) and 10.2 cm (4 in). Made by Sowerby, GATESHEAD (the
bowl bears the factory mark). The patterns were registered in 1877 and 1876,
and both pieces bear registry marks. *Tyne and Wear County Council Museums
(Shipley Art Gallery, Gateshead). See page 159*

165. Pressed BASKET of amber-coloured glass. Ht. 10.2 cm (4 in). Made by
George Davidson, GATESHEAD, and marked with serial number of
registration in 1888. *Author's collection. See page 159*

166. Pressed JUG of uncoloured glass. Ht. 12.4 cm (4.9 in). Made by George Davidson, GATESHEAD, and marked with serial number of registration in 1899. *Author's collection. See page 159*

enthusiasm of the seventies and eighties for the arts of the Far East and especially of Japan. Sowerby's produced many new designs in the years around 1880 with a freedom which was at least appropriate to the medium, even though the results are not always to be admired. Many of them were square in section, or otherwise not circular, and were raised on small feet (Plates 160–2). The relief decorations were often asymmetrical arrangements of plants (Plates 160, 161), or might even be Japanese figures. The most usual surface treatments were vertical fluting (Plates 161, 162) and an imitation of basketwork (Plate 163). Of the Sowerby examples illustrated here, three are made in plain opaque glasses (Plates 162, 163), one is in the partially opaque opalescent glass (Plate 160), and two are in the opaque marbled glasses, often known as 'slag glass', which came to be especially associated with this class of work (Plate 164). It may be noticed that although the designs of these pieces date mainly from the later seventies, the moulds would have been used over many years and the colours are not necessarily those of the dates of design.

In this phase of the history of pressed glass other manufacturers were also making use of coloured glasses. Examples are illustrated here from the Salford firm of John Derbyshire and the Gateshead firm of George Davidson, originally registered in 1876 and 1888 (Colour Plate I, Plate 165). In 1889 George Davidson was advertising a blue-shaded glass called 'Pearline', and later was making a 'primrose' glass. Coloured glasses, plain or shaded, were often used in a curious combination of free forms with would-be cut decoration. The Manchester firm of Burtles, Tate & Co., which was manufacturing the most popular sorts of table and fancy glass during the nineties, was using hand methods for many, if not most, of its fancy wares. The firm produced quantities of cheap flower stands, and in these the base dishes and fern decorations might be pressed, although the other components were hand wrought.[9] One has the impression that in spite of the frequent use of colour pressed glass was becoming less suited during the nineties to the popular conception of fancy glass, while the great revival of cut glass was enabling the pressed-glass makers to concentrate increasingly upon what they no doubt considered their normal business of imitating the effects of cutting (Plate 166).

[9] *Pottery Gazette*, Jan. 1891, Fancy Trades Supplement, p. 4.

Marks

REGISTRY MARKS

Objects made according to designs registered at the Patent Office Design Registry from 1842 to 1883 may bear a lozenge-shaped mark, by which the date of registration can be deduced from the codes (*a*) and (*b*) below. The mark also provides a key whereby other details of a registration may be obtained from official records. During this period all glassware was listed as Class III.

In 1884 a new series began which was marked on objects as a serial number, normally preceded by the letters Rd. A list of the first registrations issued in January of each year, of objects in all classes, is appended at (*c*). Before the beginning of 1892, however, account should be taken of a slight numerical overlap between the registrations of each December and January.

Registry marks appear often on pressed glass, but are only occasionally found on other types of glassware.

(*a*) 1842 to 1867

Years		Months		
1842 — X	1855 — E	January	— C	
1843 — H	1856 — L	February	— G	
1844 — C	1857 — K	March	— W	
1845 — A	1858 — B	April	— H	
1846 — I	1859 — M	May	— E	
1847 — F	1860 — Z	June	— M	
1848 — U	1861 — R	July	— I	
1849 — S	1862 — O	August	— R	
1850 — V	1863 — G	September	— D	
1851 — P	1864 — N	October	— B	
1852 — D	1865 — W	November	— K	
1853 — Y	1866 — Q	December	— A	
1854 — J	1867 — T			

(R may be found as the month mark for 1st–19th September 1857, and K for December 1860.)

(*b*) 1868 to 1883

Years		Months	
1868 — X	1876 — V	January — C	
1869 — H	1877 — P	February — G	
1870 — C	1878 — D	March — W	
1871 — A	1879 — Y	April — H	
1872 — I	1880 — J	May — E	
1873 — F	1881 — E	June — M	
1874 — U	1882 — L	July — I	
1875 — S	1883 — K	August — R	
		September — D	
		October — B	
		November — K	
		December — A	

(For 1st–6th March 1878, G was used for the month and W for the year.)

(*c*) 1884 to 1901

1884 — 1	1890 — 141273	1896 — 268392	
1885 — 19754	1891 — 163767	1897 — 291241	
1886 — 40480	1892 — 185713	1898 — 311658	
1887 — 64520	1893 — 205240	1899 — 331707	
1888 — 90483	1894 — 224720	1900 — 351202	
1889 — 116648	1895 — 246975	1901 — 368154	

FACTORY MARKS

Marks on hand-made glass are rare and usually self-explanatory. The following crests appear as trade marks on pressed glass in the latter part of the nineteenth century.

Sowerby, Gateshead

George Davidson, Gateshead

John Derbyshire, Salford

Early and late marks of Henry Greener, Sunderland

For details of these marks see C. R. Lattimore, *English 19th-Century Press-Moulded Glass*, London (1979).

Several different printed marks were used on Richardson opalines. They clearly identify the factory but do not state the full title of the firm at the time of manufacture, and they are not therefore used in the illustrations of this book as evidence of dating.

Select Bibliography

L. M. Angus-Butterworth, *British Table and Ornamental Glass*, London (1956)
Art Journal, London (1849–1912)
Art Union (monthly journal), London (1839–48)
G. W. Beard, *Nineteenth-Century Cameo Glass*, Newport (1956)
Sir Hugh Chance. 'The Donnington Wood Glasshouses', *Glass Circle Papers*
  (London), No. 140 (November 1964)
D. C. Davis and K. Middlemas, *Coloured Glass*, London (1968)
Dudley Art Gallery, *English 'Rock Crystal' Glass* (exhibition catalogue, 1976)
E. M. Elville, *English Tableglass*, London and New York (1951)
E. M. Elville, *English and Irish Cut Glass*, London (1953)
E. M. Elville, *Paperweights and Other Glass Curiosities*, London (1954)
A. Fleming, *Scottish and Jacobite Glass*, Glasgow (1938)
H. J. Haden, *Notes on the Stourbridge Glass Trade*, Brierley Hill (1949) (reprinted Dudley
  Public Libraries 1969 and 1977)
H. J. Haden, *The 'Stourbridge Glass' Industry in the 19c*, Tipton (1971)
R. and L. Grover, *Art Glass Nouveau*, Rutland, Vermont (1967)
R. and L. Grover, *Carved and Decorated European Art Glass*, Rutland, Vermont (1970)
D. R. Guttery, *From Broad-Glass to Cut Crystal*, London (1956)
P. Hollister Jr., *The Encyclopaedia of Glass Paperweights*, New York (1969)
W. B. Honey, *Glass* (Victoria and Albert Museum handbook), London (1946)
W. B. Honey, *English Glass*, London (1946)
P. Jokelson, *Sulphides. The Art of Cameo Incrustation*, New York (1968)
Journal of Design and Manufactures, London (1849–52)
C. R. Lattimore, *English 19th-Century Press-Moulded Glass*, London (1979)
Barbara Morris, *Victorian Table Glass and Ornaments*, London (1978)
J. Northwood Jr., *John Northwood*, Stourbridge (1958)
Betty O'Looney, *Victorian Glass* (Victoria and Albert Museum picture book), London
  (1972)
Apsley Pellatt, *Memoir on the Origin, Progress, and Improvement of Glass Manufactures . . .*,
  London (1821)
Apsley Pellatt, *Curiosities of Glass Making*, London (1849)
Ada Polak, *Glass: Its Makers and Its Public*, London (1975)
Pottery Gazette (initially *Pottery and Glass Trades' Review*), London (1877–   )
H. J. Powell, *Glass-making in England*, Cambridge (1923)

SELECT BIBLIOGRAPHY

A. C. Revi, *Nineteenth-Century Glass*, revised edn., New York (1967)

J. A. H. Rose, 'The Apsley Pellatts', *The Glass Circle 3*, London (1979)

Elisa Steenberg, *Svenskt Adertonhundratals Glas*, Stockholm (1953)

W. A Thorpe, *A History of English and Irish Glass*, 2 vols., London and Boston (1929)

W. A. Thorpe, *English Glass*, 2nd edn., London (1949)

Tyne and Wear County Council Museums, *Glassmaking on Wearside* (1979)

K. Vincent, *Nailsea Glass*, Newton Abbot (1975)

H. Wakefield, 'The Development of Design for Pressed Glassware, as Exemplified in British Sources', *Papers of International Congress on Glass*, No. 208, Brussels (1965)

H. Wakefield, 'Glasswares by Apsley Pellatt', *Antiques*, January 1965

H. Wakefield, 'Richardson Glass', *Antiques*, May 1967

H. Wakefield, 'The Development of Victorian Flower-stand Centrepieces', *Annales du 4e Congrès des 'Journées Internationales du Verre'*, Liège (?1968)

H. Wakefield, 'Early Victorian Styles in Glassware', in R. J. Charleston etc., *Studies in Glass History and Design*, Sheffield (1968)

H. Wakefield, 'Venetian Influence on British Glass in the Nineteenth Century', *Annales du 5e Congrès de l'Association Internationale pour l'Histoire du Verre*, Liège (1972)

H. Wakefield, 'Victorian Flower Stands', *Antiques*, August 1970

H. Wakefield, 'Glasswares at the Great Exhibition of 1851', *Annales du 7e Congrès de l'Association Internationale pour l'Histoire du Verre*, Liège (1978)

P. Warren, *Irish Glass*, London (1970); 2nd edn. London (1981)

M. S. D. Westropp, *Irish Glass*, revised edn., Dublin (1978)

G. Wills, *English and Irish Glass*, London (1968)

G. Wills, *Antique Glass for Pleasure and Investment*, London (1971)

G. Wills, *Victorian Glass*, London (1976)

H. W. Woodward, *Art, Feat and Mystery: the Story of Thomas Webb & Sons, Glassmakers*, Stourbridge (1978)

Index

References to plates are in italics

Absolon, William, 46; *33*
acid-etching, 102, 106, 124, 150; *102–5, Colour Plate A*
Adelaide, Queen, *143*
alabaster glass, 64
Albert, Prince, 74; *71, 146*
Alloa, 53; *82*
Anglo-Irish period, 20; *see also* Irish glass
Anglo-Venetian glass, 74
arched patterns, 33; *20, 21*; *see also* Gothic influence
Art Nouveau, 139
Arts and Crafts movement, 15, 133

Baccarat, 98, 143; *148*
Bacchus (Bacchus, Green & Green; Bacchus & Green; George Bacchus & Sons), 62, 68, 74, 77, 142, 147; *61, 70, 86, 149, Colour Plate B*
Badger, *9*
Baird, John 94; *94*
Bank Quay glassworks, *42*
Barbe, Jules, 124; *124, 125*
Barnes, Isaac, 113; *111*
barrel shape, 22, 29; *3, 9*
baskets, 45, 119
beads, *see* drops
Belfast, 20
Belgium, 19, 143
bell shape, 33; *84, 85*
Biedermeier, 20, 29, 60
Birmingham, 29, 143; *14–16*; *see also* Bacchus, Isaac Barnes, John Gold, Rice Harris & Son, Hukin & Heath, Lloyd & Summerfield, F. & C. Osler, Stone, Fawdry & Stone, John Walsh Walsh, *and below*
Birmingham 1849 exhibition, 62, 77, 142
Birmingham City Museum and Art Gallery, 106
Bohemia, *see* Central Europe
Bott, Thomas, 64

Boulton & Mills, 113, 119, 122
Brierley Hill, *see* Stevens & Williams, *and below*
Brierley Hill Glass Collection, 13
'Brilliant' style, 45, 94; *28–31*
Bristol, 46, 48; *see also* Isaac Jacobs, William & Thomas Powell, Henry Ricketts
British Association for the Advancement of Science, 62
British Museum, 106
Broadfield House Glass Museum, 13
broad-fluted style, 29, 33, 60, 147; *18–22*
Bromsgrove district, *see* George Ernest Fox
'Bronze' glass, 124
bucket shape, 22, 80; *8, 76, 81*
'Burmese' glass, 124; *121*
Burns, Robert, *51*
Burtles, Tate & Co., 159
busts, 74, 79, 150; *71*; *see also* sulphides

cameo glass, 98, 106, 111; *106–9, Colour Plate F*
cameo incrustations, 57; *see also* sulphides
candelabra, 117, 119
canes, 74, 77, 124; *48(b), 86(b), 87(b), Colour Plate E*
cased glass, *see* layered glass
Central Eurpe, 19, 29, 45, 60, 62, 80, 92, 94, 106, 117
centrepieces, 112, 113, 117, 130; *114*; *see also* flower stands
champagne glass, *see* saucer champagne glass
chandeliers, 119, 122
Chicago 1893 exhibition, 111
chip engraving, 86; *82*
Christy, J. F., 64, 68, 113; *60, 68, Colour Plate C*
'Clutha' glass, 133; *132, 133*
Coalport, 64
coated decoration, 53, 57; *49*
Cockhedge glassworks, *39, 48*
Cole, Henry, 68, 94; *Colour Plate C*
coloured glass, 20, 45, 46–79, 106, 112, 113, 122–39, 159
Conservatoire National des Arts et Métiers, *see* Paris

Copeland, W. T. (& Sons), 92; *91*
Cork, 20
Couper, James, & Sons, 133; *132, 133*
cribs, 130
cut decoration: 15, 19–45, 48, 57, 62, 74, 80, 102, 112, 133, 140, 147, 159; *1–31, 52; see also* layered glass, silvered glass
cylindrical shape, 29, 33; *18*

Daniell, R. P., 111
Davenport (John), 29, 53; *17, 49*
Davidson, George, 159, 161; *165, 166*
Davis, Greathead & Green, 62, 68, 142
Denby, 102
Dennis vase, *see* Pegasus vase
Derbyshire, John, 150, 159, 161; *157, Colour Plate I*
diamond cutting, 22, 29, 45; *3, 6, 10*
diamond moulding, 113, 117, 124
diamond-point engraving, 86; *81*
Dobson, J., 119
Dobson & Pearce, 92, 117, 119
Donnington Wood glasshouses, 48; *37*
doorstops, *see* dumps
Dresser, Christopher, 133; *132, 134*
drops, 113; *111, 112, 114*
drop stem, 33; *52*
Dublin, 20; *see also* Pugh glassworks
Dudley, *see* Badger, Denby, Thomas Hawkes, William Herbert, *and below*
Dudley Metropolitan Borough, 13, 64
dumps, 77; *72*

Edinburgh, 8; *see also* John Ford, A. Jenkinson
Edward, Prince of Wales, 143; *147*
Elgin vase, 106; *105*
Ellison glassworks, *see* Sowerby
Empire style, 19, 33
engraved decoration, 15, 19, 33, 37, 64, 74, 80–111, 112, 133, 150; *73–101, 105–9*
epergnes, 117, 119; *23; see also* centrepieces, flower stands
Erard, Oscar Pierre, 124; *126*
Erskine D., *82*
Escalier de Cristal, 98
etching, *see* acid-etching
Excise, Glass, 20, 22, 33, 48, 57, 60
Excise Commissioners of Inquiry, 22

fairy lights, 124
Falcon glasshouse, *see* Apsley Pellatt
fan cutting, 22; *5*
fancy glass, 15, 45, 46–79, 112–39, 159; *32–72, 110–41, Colour Plate G*
Far-Eastern influence, 98, 111, 122, 159
Fereday, J. T., *Colour Plate F*
'fern leaves', 122; *118*
fern patterns, 92, 94; *92, 93*
filigree, *see* canes
fire polishing, 142

flower centres, *see* flower stands
flower stands, 15, 117, 119, 122, 130, 159; *117, 118, 130; see also* centrepieces
flute glasses, 22, 33; *7*
Ford, John, 57, 92; *23, 51, 92, 110, 155*
Fox, George Ernest, *130*
France, 19, 45, 60, 62, 64, 77, 98, 111, 124, 143
friggers (including toys), 15, 53, 130; *46–8*
Fritsche, William, 98; *97, 98*
frosted glass, *see* ice-glass
fruit and flower glasses, *see* flower stands
furnace manipulated glass, 15, 19, 64, 133, 139

Gallé, Emile, 111
Gateshead, *see* George Davidson, Sowerby
George III, *50*
George IV, *8*
gilded decoration, 60, 64, 68, 124; *32, 33, 58, 125; see also* gold enamel ware
gimmel flasks, 48
Gladstone, 150; *158*
Glasgow, *see* John Baird, James Couper & Sons, George Walton
globular shapes, 33, 86, 117; *27, Colour Plate B*
Gold, John, 147
gold enamel ware, 57, 102; *Colour Plate A*
Gothic influence, 62, 133; *see also* arched patterns
Great Exhibition, *see* London 1851 exhibition
Greek influence, 64, 68, 86, 92, 94, 150
Green, J. G., 86, 92, 94; *88*
Green, James (& Nephew), 92, 106, 119
Greener, Henry, 150, 161; *153, 158*
Guest, T., 102
Guest Brothers, 106, 111

Hammond, E., *31*
Hancock, George, 68
Harris, Rice, & Son, 62, 74, 77, 142, 143, 147; *Colour Plate E*
Hawkes, T. G. (Corning, New York), 102
Hawkes, Thomas, 57, 86, 102, 142; *Colour Plate A*
Heppell, W. H., 150; *156*
Herbert, William, 86, 102
Herbert family, *see above*
Heriot, George, *51*
Hobbs, Brockunier & Co., *153*
Hodgetts, Joshua, 102
hollows, 33, 147; *27*
Holyrood glassworks, *see* John Ford
Hudson, Thomas, 80; *80*
Hukin & Heath, 133; *134*
Hunter, Richard, *23*
hyalith, *see* lithylin

ice-glass, 74; *69, 70*
'intaglio', 98, 102, 106; *101*
intaglio moulding, 142; *143*
iridescent glasses, 124
Irish glass, 20, 22, 29

Islington glassworks (Birmingham), *see* Rice Harris & Son

Jackson, T. G., 133; *Colour Plate H*
Jacobs, Isaac, 46; *32*
Japanese influence, *see* Far-Eastern influence
Jenkinson, A., 133
Jones, J., 92; *91*
Jubilee, *see* Queen Victoria

Keller, H., 94; *94*
Keller, Joseph, 98; *99*
Kilner, J., & Sons (Kilner Brothers), 77
Knottingley, 79
Kny, Frederick E., 94, 98; *95, 96*

lacy style, 143, 147, 150; *145–8*
Lambeth, *see* J. F. Christy
Landseer, *157*
Lane, Joseph, *39*
'latticino' decoration, 124
Launay Hautin, 143
Lawrence, Stephen, 64
layered glass, 57, 60, 62, 64, 74, 102; *53–5, Colour Plate B*
Lechevrel, Alphonse Eugène, 111; *107*
Leicester, Joseph, 139; *138*
Lerche, Emanuel, 94; *93*
Libbey Glass Company (W. L. Libbey & Son), 45; *155*
lithyalin, 60
Lloyd & Summerfield, 62, 74, 142
Locke Joseph, 111
London, 92, 117, 133; *Colour Plate A; see also* British Museum, J. F. Christy, W. T. Copeland, Dobson & Pearce, J. G. Green, James Green, Naylor & Co., Apsley Pellatt, W. P. & G. Phillips, James Powell & Sons, Royal Polytechnic Institution, Society of Arts, Victoria and Albert Museum, *and below*
London 1851 exhibition, 20, 37, 46, 57, 60, 62, 64, 68, 74, 86, 117, 119, 143; *25, 26*
London 1862 exhibition, 37, 92, 94, 112, 113, 119
London 1884 International Health Exhibition, 98
Longport, *see* Davenport

Manchester, *see* Burtles, Tate & Co., Molineaux, Webb & Co., *and below*
Manchester 1845–46 exhibition, 60
Millar, J. H. B., 92
Millar, John, 92; *110*
millefiori decoration, *see* canes
Miller, Samuel, 29
Milton vase, 106
Molineaux, Webb & Co., 150; *152*
Morris, Marshall, Faulkner & Co., *see below*
Morris, William, 133
'moss agate', 124; *128*

moulded glass, 140–59; *71, 142–66; see also* pressed glass
Mount Washington Glass Company, 124
Muckley, W. J., 64, 86; *85*
muslin glass, 133

Nailsea, 46, 48, 53, 112; *34–42*
Naylor & Co., 92, 119
Newcastle upon Tyne, 53, 80; *79; see also* W. H. Heppell, Thomas Hudson
Northwood, Charles, *108*
Northwood, J. & J., 106, 111; *103, 104*
Northwood, John, 98, 102, 106, 111, 122; *100, 105, 106, 108*
Northwood, John, jun., 13, 106

oenochoe shape, *see* Greek influence
O'Fallon, James, 98
ogee-curved profiles, 33; *87(a)*
'Old Roman' glass, 124, 133
opalescent glass, 133, 159; *119, 135, 137, 160*
opaline glasses, 60, 62, 64, 68; *56–64; see also* opalescent glass, *and below*
opaque-white glass, 46, 48, 53, 62, 106; *33, 44, 45, 122; see also* opaline glasses
Oppitz, Paul, 92; *91*
Orchard, John, 98; *99*
Orford Lane glassworks, *48*
Osler, F. & C., 37, 62, 74; *29, 71, 87(a), 89*
ovoid shapes, 92; *90, 91*

painted decoration, 46, 53, 60, 62, 64, 68, 124; *44, 45, 55–7, 59, 60, 65–8, 124, 126, Colour Plates A, C*
Pantin, Cristallerie de, 98
paperweights, 74, 77; *72, 157, Colour Plate E*
Pargeter, Philip, 106, 122
Paris 1867 exhibition, 37, 92, 113, 119, 139; *110*
Paris 1878 exhibition, 37, 98, 106, 124, 133, 139; *104, 107*
Paris, Conservatoire National des Arts et Métiers, 29
Patent Office Design Registry, 113, 119, 147, 160
'Peach' glass, 124
Pearce, Daniel, 117
'Pearline' glass, 159
Pegasus vase, 106; *106*
Pellatt, Apsley (*also* Pellatt & Green *and* Pellatt & Co.), 29, 33, 57, 68, 74, 92, 94, 140, 142; *22, 27, 50, 54, 69, 87(b), 142, 143*
Phillips, W. P. & G. (& Pearce), 92, 117, 119; *90*
Phoenix glassworks (Bristol); *10*
Phoenix glassworks (Dudley); *9*
pillar moulding, 140; *142*
pincered work, 117, 130; *116, 130*
plateaux, 102, 122
Portland vase, 106, 111
Powell, Harry J., 117, 139
Powell, James, & Sons, 74, 119, 122, 133; *115, 131, 135–41, Colour Plate H*

Powell, William & Thomas; *9*
pressed glass, 15, 37, 45, 48, 142–59; *144–66,*
    Colour Plate I
printies, *see* hollows
printing, 68, 162; *61–4, Colour Plate A*
Pugh glassworks, 94

raspberries, *see* drops
Reading, William, 143
Redgrave, Richard, 37, 68; *Colour Plate C*
Red House glassworks, *see* Philip Pargeter
Regency style, 19, 22, 29, 33, 60; *1–13*
Regent Prince, *50*
relief carving, 106; *105; see also* cameo glass
Renaissance motifs, 92
ribbing, 113, 117; *111–15*
Richardson, Benjamin, 60, 102; *102*
Richardson firm (Webb & Richardson; W. H.,
    B. & J. Richardson; Benjamin Richardson;
    Hodgetts, Richardson & Pargeter;
    Hodgetts, Richardson & Son), 37, 60, 62,
    64, 68, 86, 94, 102, 106, 111, 113, 119,
    122, 130, 142, 150, 162; *25, 26, 52, 55–9,*
    62–7, 85, 107, 112–14, 117, 118
Ricketts, Henry, *10*
Robinson & Bolton, 147; *151*
rock crystal engraving, 94, 106; *96–100*
Rococo style, 33, 147
Rousseau, Eugène, 124
Royal Polytechnic Institution, 62
ruby glass, 53, 130
rummers, 22, 80
Ruskin, John, 37
'Rusticana', 124
rusticated work, 130; *122, 129, Colour Plate G*

Salford, *see* John Derbyshire
Salviati, Antonio, 112
satin finish, 122, 124
satin glass, 124; *122, 123*
saucer champagne glass, 33, 86; *86*
Scandinavia, 117; *see also* Sweden
Schaffgotsch, Count, 119
Sheibner, Frank, *100*
shaded glass, 122, 124, 159; *121; see also*
    opalescent glass
shell components, *see* ribbing
Silesia, *see* Central Europe
silver deposit, 124; *127*
silvered glasses, 74; *Colour Plate D*
slag glass, 159; *164*
Smithsonian Institution, *see* Washington
Society of Arts, 68, 139; *138; see also below*
Society of Arts exhibition of 1849, 74, 77
Society of Arts exhibition of 1850, 68
Sowerby, 150, 159, 161; *47, 154, 160–4*
spirit stand, 45
staining, 60, 64, 86; *52(a), 83*
star cutting, 22; *5*
Stevens, James, 143

Stevens & Williams, 57, 94, 98, 102, 111, 113,
    122, 124, 130; *28, 30, 31, 99, 100, 108, 120,*
    122, 126, Colour Plate G
Stoke-on-Trent, *see* Davenport
Stone, Fawdry & Stone, 106
Stone, J. B., 106; *105*
stoppers, 22, 45, 94
Stourbridge, 57, 117, 130; *see also* Boulton &
    Mills; Davis, Greathead & Green; Guest
    Brothers; J. & J. Northwood; Philip
    Pargeter; Richardson; Joseph Webb &
    Sons; Thomas Webb & Sons; Webb &
    Richardson; Wheeley & Davis; Wood
    family, *and below*
Stourbridge Glass Collection, 13, 86
strawberry diamonds, 22; *8, 11, 12*
sulphides, 29, 57, 142; *50, 51*
Summerly's Art Manufactures, 68; *Colour Plate C*
Sunderland, 80; *76; see also* Henry Greener
Sussex, Augustus Frederick, Duke of, *11*
Sweden, 45, 143

tankard shape, 92; *92, 93*
tantalus, *see* spirit stand
'Tapestry' glass, *126*
Thomson, F. Hale, 74
threading, 74, 113; *118, 126*
three-lipped decanter, 15, 94; *95*
Tieze, Franz, 94
toys, *see* friggers
Trafalgar, *73*
trailing, 48, 64, 113, 117, 124, 130
transfer-printing, *see* printing
'Tricolor' glass, 124
Turnbull, Matthew, *159*
Tutbury Glass Company, 147, 150
twisted work, 113, 119; *103, 110, 117*

United States of America, 19, 20, 45, 111, 112,
    124, 140, 142, 143, 150; *153, 155*

Val St. Lambert, 143; *148*
Varnish, Edward, 74; *Colour Plate D*
Venetian influence, 68, 74, 112, 113, 117, 122,
    124, 133
Venice, 19, 111; *see also above*
Victoria, Queen, 74, 79, 143, 150; *144–6, Colour*
    Plate A
Victoria and Albert Museum, 13, 86, 122, 133
Vienna 1873 exhibition, 92; *91*

Wakefield, 77
Wales, Prince of, *13; see also* Edward, Prince of
    Wales
Walsh, John Walsh, 124, 130
Walton, George, 133; *133*
Warrington, 53; *see also* Bank Quay;
    Cockhedge; Orford Lane; Robinson &
    Bolton
Washington, Smithsonian Institution, 106

Waterford, 20, 22, 29
waved edges, 117, 130
Webb, Joseph, (& Son), 119, 147
Webb, Philip, 133; *131*
Webb, Thomas, & Sons, 15, 94, 98, 106, 111,
    113, 117, 122, 124, 133; *95–8, 109, 121–5,
    Colour Plate F*
Webb, Thomas Wilkes, 98, 106; *106*
Webb & Richardson, 142
wheel engraving, *see* engraved decoration
Wheeley & Davis, 142

Whitefriars glassworks; *see* James Powell
    & Sons
Wolverhampton 1884 exhibition, 98
Wood, Thomas, *see below*
Wood family, 86; *83*
Woodall, George, 111; *109*
Woodall, Thomas, 111; *Colour Plate F*
Wrockwardine Wood glasshouses, *see*
    Donnington Wood

Yarmouth, *see* William Absolon